I0704157

Chasing Forever

A Small Town Romance

Second Hope Series

Jessica Prince

Copyright © 2025 by Jessica Prince
www.authorjessicaprince.com

Published by Jessica Prince Books LLC

All rights reserved.
No part of this book may be reproduced in any form or by any electronic or mechanical means, including information storage and retrieval systems, without written permission from the author, except for the use of brief quotations in a book review.

To everyone who ever felt they weren't strong enough...
You're a badass!
You don't have to believe it just yet if you aren't ready. I'll believe it for you.

Let's Connect

By signing up for my newsletter, you're guaranteeing you'll stay up to date on all new releases, cover reveals, giveaways, sales, and all the other exciting book news I have coming!

I pinky-promise to use my emails for good only, not to spam you, and make sure each one is enjoyable for everybody.

Sign up on my website at: www.authorjessicaprince.com

Content Warning

While this story is all about finding your inner strength and falling into a deep, healthy love, there are also topics that might be sensitive to readers.

This story deals with domestic violence, both on and off the page, as well as drug abuse, so please be mindful as you dive into Tristan and Merritt's story.

A Note from the Author

If you're curious about where Tristan got his start, I've attached a little graphic below to make that easier for you.

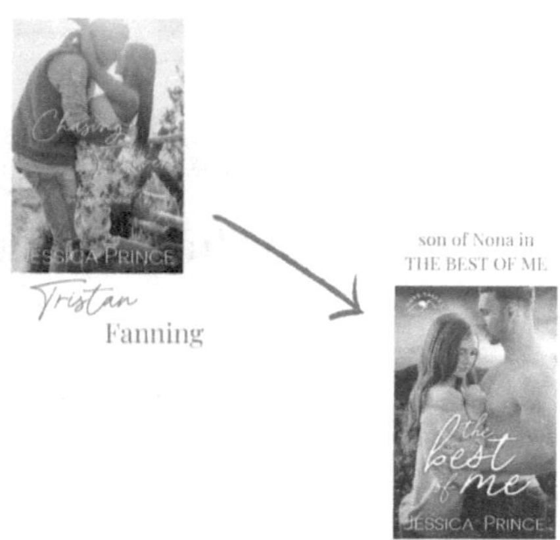

I hope you enjoy this story as much as I enjoyed writing it!

Happy reading, and all the love,
~ Jess

Discover Other Books by Jessica

SECOND HOPE SERIES
The Little Things
Tangled Up With You
Twice in a Lifetime
Chasing Forever

ASHLAND SERIES
Dead to Rights

WHITECAP SERIES
Crossing the Line
My Perfect Enemy
Turn of the Tides

THE PEMBROOKE SERIES:

Sweet Sunshine
Coming Full Circle
A Broken Soul
Should Have Been Me

<u>WHISKEY DOLLS SERIES</u>

Bombshell
Knockout
Stunner
Seductress
Temptress
Vamp

<u>HOPE VALLEY SERIES:</u>

Out of My League
Come Back Home Again
The Best of Me
Wrong Side of the Tracks
Stay With Me
Out of the Darkness
The Second Time Around
Waiting for Forever
Love to Hate You
Playing for Keeps
When You Least Expect It
Never for Him

<u>REDEMPTION SERIES</u>

Bad Alibi

Crazy Beautiful

Bittersweet

Guilty Pleasure

Wallflower

Blurred Line

Slow Burn

Favorite Mistake

Sweet Spot

<u>THE CLOVERLEAF SERIES</u>

Picking up the Pieces

Rising from the Ashes

Pushing the Boundaries

Worth the Wait

<u>THE COLORS NOVELS</u>

Scattered Colors

Shrinking Violet

Love Hate Relationship

Wildflower

<u>THE LOCKLAINE BOYS</u>

Fire & Ice

Opposites Attract

Almost Perfect

<u>CIVIL CORRUPTION SERIES</u>
Corrupt
Defile
Consume
Ravage

<u>GIRL TALK SERIES:</u>
Seducing Lola
Tempting Sophia
Enticing Daphne
Charming Fiona

<u>STANDALONE TITLES:</u>
One Knight Stand
Chance Encounters
Nightmares from Within

<u>DEADLY LOVE SERIES:</u>
Destructive
Addictive

Chapter One

Merritt

T *hen*

STANDING in front of the bathroom mirror, I double checked to make sure the bruises that speckled my body in the areas where clothes couldn't hide their existence were covered beneath the layers of concealer I'd spent fifteen minutes applying.

The one on my collarbone that would peek out from my top was perfectly concealed. The fingerprint shaped bruises on my wrist could be covered by the thick band of my smart watch, and the faded yellow and green spot at my temple was easy enough to hide with my makeup, but I'd have to make sure not to tuck my hair behind my ear, just in case.

Everything else would be hidden easily enough beneath my work uniform of light blue scrubs.

I'd gotten really good at hiding the evidence of my husband's anger. Six years of practice had turned me into a seasoned professional.

If only my gift with concealer hid the pain as well. Unfortunately, there wasn't much I could do about that other than grin and bear it. Something else I'd gotten really good at over the span of my marriage to Warren. Ibuprofen took the edge off, and that was the best I could hope for—at least without a trip to the emergency room, which was out of the question.

Blinking away the burn forming behind my eyes that made my vision foggy, I twisted to look at the place on my back that had been giving me the most trouble. Along the right side, about five inches above my hip and three inches from my spine, was a contusion perfectly shaped like the sole of Warren's shiny black loafer.

A flash of that particular fight from the night before popped into my head, and I had to squeeze my eyes shut and focus on my breathing to force back the acidic burn crawling up my throat. The crash of the plate against the tile floor, the harsh words he yelled with each blow he rained down on me, his foot on my back keeping me pinned to the ground as the shards of ceramic poked through my clothes and sliced my skin.

I carefully pulled in a steadying breath until a sharp stab shot through my midsection. I'd been down this road enough times to know that my ribs weren't broken, but they were still sore as hell, probably deeply bruised.

That was another thing I'd gotten really good at . . . cataloging my injuries. I knew when something was broken or simply sprained, when a tendon had been stretched to the max, and the symptoms of a concussion —both minor *and* severe. Those were talents I never would have thought I'd need, and I certainly never imagined I'd need those skills because of my own husband.

The man I married was supposed to love and protect me, honor and cherish me, just as I did him. I always imagined the man I married would be like the handsome, noble princes in the fairy tales I loved to watch as a little girl. He was supposed to be the one to protect me from all the evil and pain in the world, not be the cause of it.

He was supposed to be the one I was safe with, not the one who hurt me.

That burn behind my eyes sparked back to life. My nose began to sting, and I had to pinch my eyes shut against the building threat of tears. This wasn't supposed to be my life.

It was moments such as these that the hold I had on the wall I'd built in my mind slipped and memories I fought so hard not to remember crept to the forefront. Those tiny little actions that anyone could have misconstrued as someone simply having a bad day were now glaring red flags that I couldn't help but wonder how I'd missed. Looking back, the signs were there, flashing the most blinding neon, but in the moment, I hadn't seen them for what they were. I'd asked myself a million times if I was that blind, but the truth was, he was a good actor.

I knew I wasn't to blame for Warren's rage, that no matter what he said, it *wasn't* my fault that he hit me. But sometimes those intrusive thoughts were too hard to ignore, and they carried a weight that could easily drown me if I wasn't careful.

I pulled in a steadying breath through my nose and blew it past my trembling lips as I forced my eyes open once more and took in the woman standing before me. I barely recognized the reflection staring back at me. The sad, hopeless eyes, the tense shoulders and hands that were always curled into fists because there wasn't a single moment of the day where my body wasn't braced for the next outburst. My chest was a hollow cavern, my heart having shriveled smaller and smaller with every hit and cruel word. It was so small I would have worried it wasn't there at all if it didn't still beat for one singular person in my life.

A lone tear broke free and slipped down my cheek just as Warren's frame filled the doorway to the bathroom. His face scrunched with grief that I used to believe, but now saw it for the manipulation it was.

"Oh, god, baby. No." My lungs seized as he shot forward, wrapping his arms around me from behind and lowering his face to the crook of my neck. The smell of his cologne wrapped around me like a thick, suffocating blanket. The expensive scent of clean cotton and woodsy-ness made my stomach revolt, the breakfast I'd forced down only an hour ago threatening to make a reappearance.

"I'm sorry," he breathed into my skin, and it took everything to keep my top lip from curling in disgust at those familiar, pleading words. "Please don't cry, baby. I'm so fucking sorry."

But he wasn't. Not really.

I'd heard it a million times. He was sorry. He hated himself for losing control. He wished he could take it back. And the topper . . . he would never do it again.

Lies. Lies. Lies.

His arms constricted, pulling my back flush against his chest, nuzzling deeper into my neck. My skin crawled everywhere he touched. Shivers of revulsion ran through me as he peppered my shoulder and neck with kisses. "I swear to you, Merritt, it'll never happen again. Never. I mean it this time. I'll get help. I'll talk to someone; you have my word."

Those very promises kept me from leaving for so long . . . the heartfelt words spoken with such remorse, the tears that always rimmed his eyes as he took in the damage he'd caused. For *so long*, I believed he meant them; he really was sorry and wanted to get help. That he loved me as much as he claimed. But now I knew the truth. They were as empty as I was inside. Hollow words that tore another piece of me away until there was hardly anything left.

"Please say you forgive me," he begged, trailing his lips up my temple. "I love you, Mer." The way he held me sure didn't feel like love. It felt like possession. Ownership. His arms were like steel bands around my torso, one hand gripping firmly to my hip as the other held on to my arm. "I love you so much."

My chin trembled as I clenched my jaw and closed my eyes. I couldn't do this anymore. I couldn't keep living like this. Warren had already stolen so much of me that I was scared I'd wake up one day soon and there would be nothing left at all. No will, no drive, not even the smallest niggling of hope. I was terrified I'd blink and be nothing more than a shell.

"Say it back, baby," he pleaded, his breath rustling the hair at the nape of my neck as he continued to kiss my skin feverishly. I could feel what it was doing to him, the evidence of his arousal plowing into my backside, and it took everything in me not to get sick. "Tell me you still love me."

My lips refused to move, my tongue revolting at the thought of forming those words. My body literally wouldn't allow me to let that lie out.

I *had* loved him. Madly. For a time. And I thought he loved me the same way. In the beginning, the good times outweighed the bad. He couldn't seem to keep his hands off me. If we were in the same room, it never failed that I could feel his gaze tracking me the whole time. The passion between us was combustible, making it so easy to believe him when he promised he would never hurt me again. He had to mean it, right? Because he loved me so damn much.

But I learned a long time ago that obsession was different than love. It was like poison, slowly eating away at everything it touched. It ate away at my friends until there were none left, at my hobbies, at anything that took time away from *him*. It ate away at my relationship with the only family I had left until I was completely and utterly alone.

"Merritt?"

His head came up, his dark eyes meeting mine in the mirror above the sink. How was it possible for a monster to be as handsome as he was? As horrible as it made me sound, his looks had been the first thing I noticed about him, what drew me in. They were the reason I said yes when he approached me at that bar all those years ago and asked if he could buy me a drink. They were why I'd given him my number without hesitation and agreed to a first date.

Those looks had only gotten better with each passing year, but I couldn't see them anymore. All I saw was a monster.

At my silence, the contrite mask he came into the bathroom wearing slowly fell away. There was that tell-tale tick in his jaw. The tightening around his eyes and lips. "Merritt." My name came out a little rougher as his arms grew tighter, squeezing at my injured ribs and causing me to suck in a pained gasp. But despite seeing that he was hurting me, he didn't loosen his hold. "Say it."

"I—" I couldn't do it. I just couldn't. Something inside of me had broken. Maybe Warren himself had caused it, but whatever it was, I couldn't bring myself to tell him I loved him. Even knowing what would happen if I denied what he wanted.

Warren stepped back, grabbing me by my arm and

using his grip to whip me around so fast my neck snapped painfully. "Fucking *say it.*"

The mask had fallen, revealing the monster lurking beneath. The *real* Warren.

My whole body began to tremble as I tugged at my arm, trying to get free. Fear and adrenaline had dumped into my bloodstream. "Warren, let me go."

"Why do you always have to be so fucking difficult, huh? Why do you have to make such a big deal out of every little thing? I already apologized, what more do you want?" he shouted. "You push and push until I have no choice."

It was as if a switch inside me flipped with those last words. My lips parted and the words came out before I had a chance to stop them.

"I don't love you."

What came next was worse than anything before. Because for the first time since I met him, no matter how violent he was, no matter how cruel or terrifying, I still didn't give him the words he wanted. After he finished, I lay on the bathroom floor, tears spilling down my face as every inch of me throbbed with each agonizing breath I took.

A part of me feared that I would never get out. That this was all that was left of my life.

But what I didn't know, what I'd lost all faith in, was

that angels really did exist. I found that out the next day when Blythe Fanning followed me into a bathroom and saved my life.

Chapter Two

Tristan

ow

MY EYES SCANNED the file I'd put together for what felt like the millionth time. It wasn't an official file, given there wasn't an official case, but I hadn't been able to get the situation out of my head. Merritt Bell had been swirling around my mind for the past two months, and I couldn't seem to dig the dark haired, green-eyed beauty out of my head.

What happened the first time I set my eyes on her in the middle of Alpha Omega's offices was something I'd never experienced in my entire life. I wasn't even sure how to describe it. It was like being struck by lightning, leaving behind a static charge that made my skin prickle and my blood hum.

Everything surrounding that first encounter had been pure havoc. From my sister being abducted to Merritt's admission that her husband had been hurting her, there was so much I struggled to wrap my head around in those short, chaotic moments. It was a blessing that we got my sister back safe and sound, and by the time I was able to turn my mind back to the other woman who needed help, the crew from Alpha Omega was already on it.

As much as I wanted to help, I was pushed out every time I tried. As it turned out, according to my sister's boyfriend and the co-owner of Alpha Omega, Rhodes Bradbury, Merritt wasn't comfortable dealing with police. It wasn't rational how bothered I was by that. I didn't know her and she didn't know me, so I had no right to be upset. I didn't blame her for not automatically assuming my badge made me the good guy, not with how scary things were in the world lately. But this need to prove I could be trusted was something that I just couldn't wrap my head around.

It was what drove to me looking into things, even after Rhodes and the guys he worked with had found her someplace safe to get away from the piece of shit she was married to. It was why I'd started digging into the man to the point some might consider a bit obsessive. But the more I found, the bigger the knot that had formed in my stomach when she said her husband's abuse had grown. On paper, the man looked like a modern-day saint. Charming and charismatic. He was a philanthropist who donated hefty amounts of his paychecks to charities for the police, fire department, and the county women's shelter. He volunteered at places like Hope House, the local children's home that had been started by my buddy Zach's parents years ago. He was pictured reading to elementary-aged kids, serving meals at a local soup kitchen, and helping to rebuild the Hennessey family's barn when a fire had left the original structure a pile of ashes.

There wasn't a single blemish on the guy's record anywhere, not even so much as a speeding ticket. From the outside, he looked like a standup guy who would do anything for his community.

That was the problem. Call me jaded, but no one was *this* good. I would have been skeptical of the man's saint-like status even if I didn't know he liked to take his hands to his wife behind closed doors.

It didn't take long for me to realize why Merritt had been so against law enforcement intervening. Back when I was a kid, Hope Valley PD had struggled with corrupt cops within their ranks, but that poison had been plucked out at the root a long time ago, and our captain, Hayes Walker, my father's best friend and former partner, ran a clean ship.

It wasn't cops themselves that Warren Bell aligned himself with. He'd taken it a step farther. He was golf buddies with more than a few judges and had grown up running in the same circle with our town's current mayor and other officials who held no small amount of power. He was insulated in a way that a small-town detective such as myself couldn't touch him. Which left a foul taste in my mouth.

Rhodes had given me what little he had to help me form a clearer picture—including the photographs his team had taken of Merritt's injuries—all of which I'd placed in the file I was slowly building.

Every time I looked at those pictures, I bounced between two feelings—red-tinged anger and gut-wrenching nausea. Knowing what that piece of human garbage had done to her made me feel downright violent at times.

I'd been so entrenched in thoughts of Merritt and the file I'd been piecing together that I hadn't heard my partner come up behind me until he clapped me on the shoulder and moved to take a seat at the desk butted up to the front of mine. "What's got you so focused over there?" Harrison asked as he kicked back in his chair and propped his booted feet on his desk. "We catch another case?"

I slapped the folder shut and slid it into the top drawer of my desk. "Nah, just a personal thing. No big deal."

Harrison silently arched a brow, knowing me well enough to know I was holding something back, but he didn't push. I trusted my partner with my life, and usually, he would have been the first person I went to with what I knew, but I couldn't shake the feeling that telling him was a betrayal of sorts. It wasn't my secret to share. Hell, I wasn't even supposed to be investigating. I just couldn't seem to help myself where Merritt was concerned.

"Whatever you say, brother." He took a sip of coffee from the mug in his hand before adding, "Just know, if it's anything you need help with, I'm here, just ask."

"I do. And I will." *If I can*, I tacked on mentally.

It wasn't like this was an actual issue. At least not any longer. Merritt was gone. Living her life somewhere else, free of the monster who had hurt her. She was probably never coming back.

I rubbed at the dull ache in the center of my chest. Christ, why did it start to hurt every time that thought popped into my head?

A pained groan vibrated from my partner's chest, pulling me out of my own head. "Ah hell. It's too early for this shit. Better brace, my man. Shit's about to hit the fan."

I lifted my gaze to Harrison, my brows pulling together. "What's—" The rest of the question died on my tongue as I twisted in my chair and spotted who was stomping up the steps into the bullpen. *Son of a bitch.*

Harrison was right. It really was too damn early to be dealing with Sue Ellen Mayfield. Not that there was ever a good time to have to deal with the pit viper or her particular brand of bullshit. That woman had been a blight on this town since I was a kid, and she had only gotten worse with age, at least according to my mom and all her friends.

The other detectives and uniformed officers in the bullpen either hunkered down, pretending to be engrossed in their work, or took off in the opposite direction. Even Harrison. The bastard hunched closer to his monitor, eyes scrunched as he studied the screen like whatever he was suddenly staring at held the answer for world peace.

Cowards.

With a resigned sigh, I rose from my chair and pinned a polite smile on my face. "Ms. Mayfield." I tried to recall if her last name was currently hyphenated, or if she was between husbands once again, but I couldn't remember. The woman ran through marriages like a stomach virus in an elementary classroom. It was impossible to keep up. "To what do we owe the honor?"

"You know good and well why I'm here," she snapped, stopping five feet in front of me and slamming her hands down on her hips. Her mouth was pinched tight into her ever-present unhappy pucker that no amount of Botox could fill out as she narrowed her eyes at me. "I have been complaining for *months* about my neighbors, and not a single one of you can bring yourselves to get off your lazy behinds to take care of it."

The woman once worked at the front desk as a receptionist *years* ago, and because of that, felt she had the right to barge in and start making demands whenever the mood struck. And the mood struck often, unfortunately.

I inhaled a deep breath as I pinched the bridge of my nose. "Ms. Mayfield," I started as calmly as I could, trying to keep the exasperation out of my voice. "I've told you several times already, if you want to make an official complaint, you need to go through the proper channels. You can't just come in here barking demands whenever you feel like it. That's not how things work. And I've also told you there is nothing the department can do for you simply because you don't like your neighbors."

"What if I were to tell you that I thought one of them was selling drugs out of their house?"

I arched a single brow, already knowing that wasn't the case. "Do you actually believe that?" I challenged, lifting a single finger to cut her off and added, "And please keep in mind, Ms. Mayfield, it's against the law to file a false police report."

Her glare intensified. I wasn't sure how she could see anything given how narrow the slits between her eyelids were. 'Should have known I couldn't depend on you to serve and protect unbiasedly . . . given who your *mother* is," she sneered.

I might have taken her dig personally if she hadn't, at one time or another, pissed off nearly every person in this town. Sue Ellen Mayfield wasn't exactly popular in Hope Valley, especially with my parents and their inner circle of friends.

I braced my feet and crossed my arms over my chest. "The fact remains, your neighbors haven't done anything illegal, and you know it." The only thing they'd done was band together in an effort to make the miserable woman's life even more difficult in the hopes that she'd eventually move away. They made sure to keep everything above board, though, acting more like nuisances than criminals. "Maybe you should look at the fact that you are the only person on that block with any sort of problem and figure out why that is. From where I'm standing, the answer seems pretty clear."

Sue Ellen's gaze shot over my shoulder, directing a withering look at my partner when he let out a snort of suppressed laughter. If it was possible, her features pinched up even more, to the point I worried she might swallow her own face. "Well, I *never*—"

"We all know that's a damn lie."

My head swiveled around at the new voice, and I had to tamp down the desire to smile as Captain Walker joined the fray. Age hadn't done much to tone down the fierceness years of military and police service had instilled in the man. He was practically family, but that didn't mean he took it easy on me . . . or anyone, for that matter. He expected the same level of dedication from all his officers, no matter their rank. The same level he put into the job day in and day out. Where other people in his position used to play the politics game, Hayes made it clear he couldn't give a shit what the local politicians thought of how he ran the department. It was his job to uphold the law and protect the citizens, not pander to them. It was one of the many reasons he made such a good captain and why he had the respect of all of us who worked under him.

Hayes stood behind me, lifting his hands to brace them on his waist, the move drawing attention to the badge and gun clipped at his hip. He was wearing that intimidating-cop face of his that used to make my balls draw up into my stomach when I was younger and got into trouble for something stupid.

"What've I told you about stormin' into my bullpen, Sue Ellen?" he asked, his voice only a few steps up from a growl. Like I said, my mom's crew weren't fans of Sue Ellen. Apparently there wasn't an age restriction on being a mean girl—though, the older she got, the more pathetic it looked—and each one of them had been targets of her particular brand of nasty more than a few times, including Hayes's wife, Temperance.

"Well, I wouldn't have to storm into anything if your officers weren't cherry-picking who they choose to help."

The vein in Hayes's forehead began to pulse, and I took a cautious step to the side. "There isn't a single officer under my command who would ignore a viable threat. Keyword there being *viable*. But I'm not wasting their time or taxpayer dollars on a whiny, entitled brat throwin' a hissy fit. Which is *exactly* what you are and what you're doin'. You have a problem with me callin' it like it is, file a complaint. In the meantime, next time you set foot past that front desk without permission, I'll personally make sure you're given a very thorough, very *long* tour of one of our holding cells. You understand me?"

I had to curl my lips between my teeth to keep from laughing out loud, but from the snorts and snickers around the bullpen, not everyone around me was as successful.

Sue Ellen's face turned a violent shade of red before she snapped, "Oh, you can rest assured I'll be filing a complaint against you. Against this whole department! We'll see what the mayor thinks about this," she barked, waving a finger in an arch over her head. "See how long you keep your cushy position then."

One corner of Hayes's mouth kicked up in a smirk. "You got me shakin' in my boots, Sue Ellen," he deadpanned. "Now do us all a favor and see your way out."

I waited until she cleared the bullpen before letting my smile loose and turning back to Hayes. "Appreciate you comin' down here to assist, Cap."

"Not a day I'll turn down the chance to put that one in her place, but that isn't why I'm down here. Got a case for you two," he said, pointing between me and Harrison. "Got an OD down at the hospital. Same cocktail as the ones you worked in the fall."

"Shit," I hissed, reaching up to massage the back of my neck. Hope Valley was a good place, a safe place for the most part, but that didn't mean we were immune to the bad shit that was out there. Drugs had been an issue on and off for our county for a long time now, but it was only recently that we started seeing overdoses with this particular mix of heroin and fentanyl. It was only a handful, and in every case, the person hadn't made it.

"That's what?" Harrison turned to look at me. "Number six? Hard to figure out who's selling this shit when every one of 'em ends up in the morgue."

"Not this time," our captain said. "This time the guy lived. You guys might just have a shot at figuring out who's behind this after all.

The two of us started out of the bullpen when the captain called out, "Guy had a kid in the house with him. That's why medical responders were able to get to him so fast. The boy saw his father go down, so keep that in mind, yeah? CPS is already on their way."

I nodded, understanding what Hayes was saying without using the actual words. There was a reason he'd assigned this case to Harrison and me. I'd only been twelve when my own father's issues with drugs marked me. If there was anyone in this department who might understand what this kid was going through, it was me.

Chapter Three

Merritt

My stomach churned as I pressed harder on the accelerator, urging my car to go faster. My fingers clenched the steering wheel so tight the leather creaked beneath my grip. My eyes darted to my ring finger as I turned the wheel, caught off guard once again by how light my left hand felt without the piece of jewelry that had been more of an albatross than a symbol of love. It had been two months since I took that ring off, and as much as I loved being free of the shackles it represented, I was still getting used to it.

I pushed away thoughts of the obnoxiously large diamond I'd never really liked and focused on the here and now. I'd been in a state of panic since getting the call that my brother was in the hospital due to a drug overdose.

It broke my heart that Ozzy had slipped . . . again, but it would have been a lie to say I wasn't surprised. Because of his drug abuse, my brother and I hadn't been very close in quite some time. The only reason I hadn't cut him out of my life for good was because of his son, Levi. As much as I might have wanted to write Ozzy off completely, it would have meant losing the connection with my little guy, and that wasn't possible.

Levi was only seven years old, and he deserved so much better than what he'd been born into. That little boy had become the most important person in my whole world the moment he was born, and leaving him behind when Rhodes and his team at Alpha Omega helped me get away from Warren was the hardest thing I'd ever done. Most days it felt like someone had reached inside my chest and ripped my heart right out. There wasn't a second that passed where I didn't miss Levi like I would a limb, but I had to get out. That had been my only shot, and as badly as I'd wanted to take Levi with me, there was no way Ozzy would have let that happen. His own son was nothing more to him than a pawn he could use against me whenever he needed money.

And I'd been the sucker who enabled him every single time. All to keep that contact with Levi.

As much as it pained me to admit, I wouldn't have gone back to Hope Valley for Ozzy—but for Levi . . . well, I'd walk right back into the lion's den for him.

And that was exactly what I was doing. As soon as the voice on the other end of the phone told me that my nephew would be placed in foster care if I didn't come to take temporary guardianship as his only other living relative, I walked out of the coffee shop in Baltimore, where I'd been working as a barista, packed up what little I had in the small studio apartment I'd been living in since Rhodes helped me relocate, and made the three and a half hour drive back to the town I had hoped never to return to. But there wasn't anything I wouldn't do for Levi.

Between bouts of panic, I'd used the long drive to call Blythe Fanning, the first person to ever offer to help me and the only real friend I'd had in far too long. She must have heard the panic in my voice, because she didn't hesitate to jump in and help as soon as I finished telling her what was going on.

A tremor worked its way down my spine as I passed the sign welcoming me to Hope Valley, but I pushed the fear down and kept going. Levi needed me.

By the time I pulled up in front of Hope House, the local children's home where they were keeping Levi until I could get to him, Blythe was already there. As soon as I parked, she was at my door, pulling it open and wrapping me in a tight embrace the moment my feet hit the ground.

The action took me by surprise, and it took a few seconds for my limbs to unfreeze. As sad as it was to admit, even to myself, I wasn't used to being hugged. At least in a way that wasn't followed by violence or manipulation. The last person to hug me with any real kindness was Levi. I could still feel the steel grip his arms had formed around my neck as I cradled him to me, tears leaking from both our eyes. As much as it hurt at the time, I hadn't been able to leave town without telling him goodbye.

That had been the worst moment of my life. Far beyond any of the pain or sadness Warren ever inflicted. I'd done my best to explain why I was leaving without going into all the ugly details he was too young to hear, and once I finished, my little guy lifted his chin and told me he hated the thought of me being sad, and if going away made me happy, that was what he wanted. That was a memory I'd held tight to over the past couple of months, one that hurt as much as it healed every time I recalled it.

I finally got myself together enough to return Blythe's embrace.

"Are you okay?" she asked once she pulled back, taking hold of my arms. Her eyes sparked with concern, and seeing that someone actually cared about me made mine begin to sting with tears I was trying desperately to keep a hold on.

I sniffled, shaking off the wave of emotion. I couldn't imagine what Levi had gone through, being the only one there when his father overdosed on heroin. Having to be the one to call the police . . . at *seven*. It broke my heart and made me so angry I wanted to track Ozzy down and beat him senseless for doing that to his son.

I couldn't understand, and I sure as hell wasn't okay. I wouldn't be until my nephew was in my arms. "I just want to see Levi. I need to get to him."

She nodded, understanding written all over her face. She had two kids of her own, after all. If there was anyone who understood, it was her. "Then let's go get him."

I turned toward the building and froze after only two steps, tipping my head back to stare up at the sign. My throat suddenly felt too tight as the reality of everything that had happened over the past several hours finally sank in fully.

"It's okay," Blythe assured me, giving my back a sympathetic pat. "I know there are all kinds of horror stories about group homes, but this place isn't like that, I swear. Levi's safe in there. I know the people in charge of this place. The director and the couple who founded it are close family friends. This is a nice, clean, safe place. Levi's okay."

"I never should have left him," I said, my quiet statement breaking in the middle of the sentence as guilt crashed into me. The hold I had on my emotions snapped and tears started to trail silently down my face.

Blythe stepped in front of me. "Hey, don't think like that. You can't blame yourself. You did what you had to do."

The knot in my throat grew bigger. "I knew I shouldn't leave him behind. I *knew* it. I should have tried harder to get him away from my brother. I should have taken him and run."

"Don't think like that. You can't do that to yourself."

"But if I had been here—"

She shook her head and held up her hand, cutting me off. "If you had been here, there's no telling the state you would be in. Those bruises . . ." She trailed off, momentarily squeezing her eyes closed and swallowing thickly. "Merritt, you were in such bad shape," she started again, her voice much quieter. "There's no telling what he would have done to you if you had stayed—how much worse it would have gotten. If you would have even . . ." Her voice broke. "If you would have survived the next time, or the time after that."

Her eyes went glassy, the sight of her fighting back her own tears making my chin quiver that much worse. My throat ached as I tried to swallow, emotion clogging it. "You had to save yourself in order to make sure you were strong enough for something just like this," she continued. "You had to heal so you could be what that little boy needs at this very moment."

I pulled in a deep breath, searching for the calm I would need before I saw Levi. The painful truth was, I hadn't been in a place to take care of Levi before. I couldn't have taken him from one monster only to trap him with another.

And speaking of that particular monster, I hadn't let myself think about what it meant to be back in the same town he was in. I would have been lying if I said I wasn't scared, but there was a voice in the back of my head—one that hadn't been there before—telling me I could do this. I was ready. I could be what Levi needed, and when it came to a potential confrontation with Warren, well, that was a bridge I would cross when I got there.

I pulled in a stuttered breath before steeling my spine and starting forward once more. The moment we crossed the threshold we were greeted by an older woman with kind eyes and a soft smile that instantly worked to ease some of my anxiety.

"Ms. Bell?"

"Yeah, hi." I reached out and took her hand, giving it a shake. "Call me Merritt."

Her gaze caught on Blythe, coming in right behind me, and I registered the surprise on her face a moment before her smile grew even wider.

"This is a nice surprise, sweetheart," she said to Blythe as she came to a stop beside me. Her eyes bounced between the two of us. "Do you guys know each other?"

Blythe leaned in and gave the woman a quick peck on the cheek before looping her arm through mine in a show of solidarity. "Yeah. We're friends." She said it with such casual ease that something warm bloomed in my chest and spread out through my limbs.

"I'm glad you're here then." The woman turned her kind eyes back to me. "Merritt, I'm Tessa Dixon. I'm the director here at Hope House. If you'll follow me, I'll take you to Levi. He's playing board games with some of the other kids in the common room."

My heart began to race as I followed Tessa through the large entry and down a long hallway to the left. My hands clenched into fists, my nails digging into the heels of my palms as anxiety squeezed at my chest.

As if reading my mood, Blythe grabbed my hand and forced my fingers straight so she could hold on. "Hey, it's going to be all right."

I nodded, inhaling deeply through my nose as I struggled to find my calm. The sound of laughter and voices grew louder the closer we got to the common room, the noise reaching a crescendo as we turned into the large open room. Kids of different ages circled a table off to our left, some with their hands thrown up in victory while others groaned in defeat. And right there in the fray was my little guy.

My heart stuttered and the air expelled from my lungs at the sight of him. I wasn't sure what I'd been expecting, but the fist that had been clenching my chest since getting that phone call instantly released as I watched Levi beam up at the older boy standing beside him and lift his hand to give the kid a high five.

"He totally sunk your battleship, bruh!" the other kid cheered on behalf of my nephew as he pointed across the table.

A smile of relief turned the corners of my mouth up just as Levi turned his head and spotted me.

"Aunt Merri!" he shouted, breaking away from the group and running full speed in my direction.

I crouched as he closed in, catching him in my arms as he launched himself. I let out an *oof* at the impact, surprised at how much bigger he'd gotten in the two months since I'd last seen him. I wrapped my arms around him and lifted him off his feet, a pang hitting me square in the heart at how much heavier he'd gotten. It wouldn't be much longer before I wasn't strong enough to pick him up. But for the time being, I was determined to ignore the strain in my arms and hold on tight.

He pulled back, his eyes glittering with excitement despite everything he'd gone through over the past several hours. "Did you see? I beat Carson in Battleship!"

"I saw," I said with a small laugh, shooting up a thank you to whatever higher power was looking down for giving my boy such resilience. Holding Levi in, I finally felt like I could take a full breath, and I filled my lungs with the scent of Levi's familiar shampoo. "That's 'cause you're the Battleship king, little dude."

Someone cleared their throat off to the side, drawing my attention. I twisted my head, my eyes going wide as soon as they locked onto the intense sky-blue gaze of the man who had been taking up way too much of my head-space over the past several weeks.

Tristan Fanning stood a few feet away, dressed in a pair of slacks and a light blue button-down shirt, his badge gleaming from its place on his belt.

I told myself countless times I'd built him up in my

head to be something bigger than he really was, that he wasn't as handsome as my mind was trying to convince me. I'd blamed it on the adrenaline and chaos swirling around that very first encounter, but as I stared at him, I knew I was in big trouble.

Because I realized what I remembered didn't come close to doing him justice.

Chapter Four

Tristan

As soon as Merritt turned the corner and stepped into the common room, my heart began to pump at a frantic pace, like it had just been shot up with pure adrenaline. She was the very last person I'd been expecting to see, and once the shock of it wore off, panic came racing on its heels. What was she doing here? Didn't she know it wasn't safe? Had she gone back to her abusive bastard of a husband? A thousand questions swirled through my mind at lightning speed. Then I noticed the way Levi's entire face lit up at the sight of her. He'd gone on and on about Aunt Mary for the past few hours, but I was just realizing that his Mary was short for Merritt . . . Merri.

Fuck.

She was his aunt. The only other living relative. And

she had to come back to make sure her nephew didn't end up in the system because his own father was a piece of shit.

My chest tugged as I watched her crouch to catch him just as he threw himself into her arms, and the way her face crumpled up like she was finally holding the missing piece of something important as her arms wound around the boy and hauled him up. The love and affection those two had for each other was written in every cell of their bodies.

That sense of being struck by lightning hit me again, just as it had the first time I laid eyes on her, and the most ridiculous thought of *mine*, pounded in my brain with every beat of my heart. It was ludicrous. I didn't even know this woman. I had no business thinking about how I wanted to keep her.

I cleared my throat, the collar of my shirt suddenly feeling too tight, and when her gaze shot up to mine, it was a wonder it didn't knock me right on my ass. Her eyes were even more beautiful than I remembered. Her irises were a pale sage, but the outer rim had a band several shades darker, a deep green that reminded me of all those times I'd lay on my back in the woods behind my mom's house and stare at the sky through the thick canopy of lush leaves.

Just one look and I was struck dumb. My lips had

parted to say . . . something, but no words came out. It wasn't exactly the best look for a police detective, but something about the woman short-circuited my brain every time I saw her. Instead of being able to behave like a normal human being that had been raised in society, I'd reverted to some sort of caveman, only able to communicate through grunts and huffs.

I'd grunted my way through a cursory greeting that Tessa initiated before deciding silence was my best bet. At least until I could get my shit together enough to function like a normal person.

I counted myself lucky that Harrison had stayed behind at the hospital. If my partner had been there to see me make an ass of myself, I'd never had heard the end of it. He wanted to be there to interview the dad whenever he finally regained consciousness. Meanwhile, I'd stuck close to the kid. It wasn't a surprise he'd been scared out of his mind after what had gone down, and something about him pulled at my center, sparking a protective instinct inside of me.

He'd shut down all the other adults back at the hospital, including the social worker from Child Protective Services. No one could get a word out of him. But for whatever reason, he seemed comfortable with me, so I stayed by his side, holding tightly to his hand the whole way from the hospital to Hope House. Fortunately, it hadn't taken long for Tessa and the other staff members to pull Levi from his shell, and even though he seemed okay, I hadn't been able to leave him.

I told myself I would stick around long enough to make sure this aunt he'd been raving about was solid, and she'd take good care of him, then I'd leave. Instead of doing that and meeting up with Harrison back at the station to debrief, I was currently standing in Tessa's office with her, Merritt, the social worker, Annabeth Kline, and my older sister, the latter who kept casting curious looks in my direction every few minutes. But I was doing my best to ignore her as I stood propped against the back wall and listened to the other two women walking Merritt through everything that would happen with her taking temporary custody of her nephew, and what the state would expect of her to make sure he was safe.

I watched her closely; I couldn't miss the way her hands clenched into fists so tight her knuckles bleached of color. Or the way the pulse in her neck fluttered wildly in time with the tick in her jaw. I also didn't miss the way the natural pink flush of her cheeks faded and she paled as they spoke of how she would have to remain local so as not to disrupt Levi's life more than it already had been, and so they could ensure she could provide a strong, stable environment.

I didn't need to be inside her head to know what had her growing pale and causing her foot to jiggle anxiously. I could see the fear she was trying desperately to hide from everyone in the room, and witnessing her strength made my chest tighten like my ribs were trying to squeeze all the air out of my lungs. Christ, she had to have been terrified to be back in the same town as that son of a bitch, but she'd done it anyway, all for her nephew.

It made me want to track Warren Bell down and beat him senseless.

Annabeth was saying something about suitable living arrangements when I noticed Merritt's eyes flare wide, panic suddenly flickering in the soft green.

"If you have an address you can provide, I can set up a home visit," Annabeth continued, oblivious to the way Merritt's shoulders were slowly creeping up around her ears.

The panic and desire to chase away the shadows stretching along her delicate features had me blurting out, "They'll be staying with me." The words spewed past my lips before my brain had a chance to engage.

Four pairs of eyes shot in my direction, ranging from curiosity from Tessa, who was practically like an aunt to Blythe and me, to utter bewilderment from my sister, to shock and even *more* panic from Merritt.

I honestly couldn't blame her, I was a complete stranger. And I could admit that my announcement was more than a little unexpected. Some—like my sister and partner—might have even said unhinged. But the words were already out there, I couldn't take them back now.

"Wait. What? I-I don't—" Merritt began to sputter before the words died off, leaving her in slack-jawed silence.

Annabeth looked in my direction. "And the address for your residence?"

I spouted off my address so she could scribble it on the legal pad in her lap.

I did my best to ignore my sister's eyes drilling into the side of my head, but the intensity finally got to be too much, and I turned to meet her gaze.

What the hell was that? She mouthed and bugged out her eyes as the meeting continued on around us.

I shrugged, not having an answer.

Blythe's gaze ping-ponged between me and Merritt, who was sitting stiff in her chair, like a marble statue. She jerked her chin toward the door and gave me that big sister glare she'd perfected when we were still kids.

I shook my head, trying to blow her off, but I should have known better. She jerked her chin again, but this time, she stabbed her elbow into my side for good measure.

I did my best to muffle my grunt of pain and shot her a scowl that promised retribution, but I still started for the door like she was basically demanding.

"Christ, B." My brows pulled into a deep frown as I rubbed at where she'd jabbed me. "I think you might have cracked a rib."

She rolled her eyes and blew out a raspberry. "Oh, you're fine, you big baby. Now stop pouting and tell me what the he—" She stopped and looked around, remembering there were kids all over the place. "Heck is going on."

Reaching up, I rubbed at the back of my neck, trying to figure it out myself. "I don't know," I confessed. "It just kind of came out."

Her brow furrowed. "I don't get it. Do you guys know each other or something?"

I shook my head. "No," I answered, knowing my reply would only confuse her more. I knew the feeling, because the irrational way I felt about Merritt confused the hell out of me as well.

Blythe's brows shot up toward her hairline. "Okay. Then . . . what the hell are you doing?" she hissed. "You can't stand having people in your space. You were two steps from a drinking problem and a permanent eye twitch when the kids and I were staying with you."

"I wasn't that bad," I insisted dryly.

She scrunched her lips to the side as if to say *you're so full of shit.* "Really? When I told you we were moving in with Rhodes, you almost pulled your hamstring, racing up the stairs to 'assist us in packing'." She added finger quotes on my words that she was using to mock me.

I blew out a raspberry and rolled my eyes. "Please. You're exaggerating."

She let out a bark of laughter. "So it *wasn't* you hurling our luggage across the front lawn like a freaking shot-putter, trying to get it as close to Rhodes's car as possible?"

Okay, so she had me there. I might have been a little overzealous in my efforts to help them . . . get the hell out of my house.

"You have a point. Whatever," I grumbled. "But in my defense, Avett kept barging into the bathroom when I was in the shower," I said, speaking of my nephew, "and Ainsley hit me in the dick so many times I don't know if it's possible for me to have kids."

Blythe failed to mask her snort. "My baby girl is excitable. She was just happy whenever you came home. It's not her fault her head only comes up to your . . . crotch . . . uh, region."

Jesus Christ. I couldn't believe we were talking about this. "Anyway, that's all beside the point," I said, steering the conversation in a different direction. "I don't mind people being in my house, and Merritt needs a place to stay. I'm only trying to help her out."

Blythe's eyes narrowed as she scrutinized me like she could see inside my head. Just as I was starting to feel twitchy, her head jerked back and her eyes bulged out. "Oh. My. God." Her gasp was so big I worried there wouldn't be enough oxygen in the building for everyone else. "You *like* her!"

"Don't be ridiculous."

"You do!"

I looked around to make sure no one had overheard. "Christ, can you keep your voice down? And stop smiling like that. You look deranged, and it's creeping me out."

She curled her lips between her teeth, but that only served to make her look like her head was seconds away from exploding, shooting glitter and rainbows all over the damn place.

I reached up to pinch the bridge of my nose, trying how to best explain a situation I didn't even understand myself. "Look, it's not what you think," I started.

Blythe's brow furrowed in confusion. "So, you don't like her?"

"No. Yes. Fucking hell," I grunted, raking a hand through my hair in frustration. "Jesus, I don't know. I don't know what the hell I feel. All I know for sure is that I'll do anything to keep that woman in there safe. And I know that makes me sound like some kind of psychopath, but I don't seem to have any control over it."

My sister reached out and wrapped her fingers around my forearm. "No, it doesn't make you sound like a psychopath." She paused. "Well . . ."

"Blythe," I growled.

She smacked me in the shoulder. "I'm kidding; will you relax? Look, I get it," she assured me. "I saw those bruises on her and I about lost it. And you've had this protective instinct ingrained in you since we were kids. I'm not surprised you'd want to help her and her nephew. Just . . . just make sure you know what you're doing, okay? Protect her, but also make sure to watch your back. Her ex is a really bad dude."

I knew better than she could imagine. "I promise." But what I didn't mention was that this whole conversation wouldn't matter if I couldn't get Merritt to agree to stay with me. I had to hope my big sister would help me with that.

Chapter Five

Merritt

I couldn't believe I was doing this. I had to have lost my damn mind somewhere between Baltimore and Hope Valley and was just realizing it. That had to be the only explanation for why I'd agreed to Tristan Fanning's offer to let Levi and me stay with him.

The refusal had been right there, on the tip of my tongue, but then Blythe vouched for her brother, waxing on about all of his good qualities. I was still on the fence, but she managed to shove me the rest of the way over by pointing out that Levi and I would be safe with him. I was leery of police and other public officials in our small town, given Warren's reach. But my gut was telling me Tristan wasn't like that.

"There isn't anything my little brother wouldn't do to protect someone under his care," she'd insisted vehe-

mently, and her eyes told me she believed that to her core. She trusted her brother. And I trusted her, so I took a leap of faith. I said yes before I had a chance to think twice, before I could start second-guessing all the reasons why it was such a terrible idea. Before I had a chance to back out, Tristan mentioned he had a dog, and that basically sealed our fate.

Truth was, there weren't a whole lot of options when it came to places to live. I needed a home for Levi, but I didn't have the money for a down payment on an apartment, and I'd just quit my job. Walking out without so much as a word, I seriously doubted I could put them down as a reference. I needed a roof over Levi's head and a job, and I needed them *now*.

Levi had been talking about Tristan's dog nonstop since we left the center, asking all kinds of questions I couldn't possibly have the answer to.

"Do you think it's a big dog, or a little dog? Do you think it'll let me snuggle with it? I bet it licks my face!" he said with an excited giggle. Through the rearview mirror I could see him bouncing around in his booster seat like he was coming out of his skin. Seeing him so excited about something after what he'd been through soothed a place inside of me that had been running off stress and anxiety for the past several hours.

As good as it felt to see that the most important

person in my life wasn't indelibly scarred by what he'd witnessed, I still wanted to track my brother down and hold a pillow over his face until his body stopped thrashing. I would never understand how a parent could do that to their own flesh and blood, and I would never forgive Ozzy for putting Levi in such a dangerous situation. No kid should have to call the police because his father was seizing and choking on his own vomit. Fortunately, that rage had been somewhat tempered by Levi's smile before I could do something stupid, like drive to the hospital and maim my older brother.

"I'm not sure. I don't see why not. And I bet it does," I said, answering his questions in order.

"If it licks my face, that means it likes me, right? You think it'll like me?"

My eyes shot back up to the mirror, my gaze landing on that precious little boy. His hair flopped down over his forehead, the color the same deep, dark brown as mine, only a few shades from black. His cheeks were still a little chubby and always had a rosy hue to them that only added to the sweet innocence in his cherubic face.

"What are you talking about? Of course, it'll like you!"

"Think so?"

"Absolutely. You're the most likable kid in the whole entire universe, little dude."

His eyes, just a tad darker green than mine, went wide and his lips parted, forming an adorable little O. "Wow, that's a whole lot."

I nodded seriously. "Sure is. I mean, think about it, kid. Every single person who's ever met you has instantly fallen in love with you."

His cute little face scrunched up in thought for a few seconds before he nodded earnestly. "Yeah. You're right. I have a *ton* of friends."

I choked out a snort. He wasn't being conceited or vain—he didn't have it in him—he was simply pointing out the truth. Most of the kids in his class gravitated toward him because he showed kindness and acceptance to everyone equally. I'd never met a human being with a bigger heart and a larger capacity to care as much as my nephew, and I counted my blessings that my brother's influence hadn't rubbed off on him.

Now it was my job to make sure Ozzy never had the chance to tarnish Levi's tender soul ever again.

"Dang straight, you do. So any dog you meet is going to love you just the same."

Levi's eyes pointed out the window beside him as his feet swung back and forth. "I always wanted a dog," he said, his voice quiet and his tone almost wistful.

I swallowed, a ball of emotion clogging my throat. "Well then this is your lucky day, isn't it? We just have to pack up the rest of your things and you'll be good to go."

I shifted my focus a bit higher in the mirror, seeing that Tristan's big gunmetal gray suburban was still trailing behind us.

When we left Hope House, he'd insisted on coming along to help. When I tried to refuse, his jaw ticked as he ground his back molars together before his features gentled.

His throat worked on a swallow as he stepped closer and lowered his voice so only I could hear. "I'm so sorry, but . . . it's still an active crime scene." The words sounded like they were being pulled roughly from his throat, almost like he didn't want to let them out but had no choice.

My eyes went wide as realization settled in, chilling me to my very bones. "You think there could be more drugs in there?"

His hand came out, his rough fingers somehow gentle as he gave my forearm a reassuring squeeze. "We don't know, but I always prefer to err on the side of caution, and I hate the thought that you and Levi could be walking into something dangerous."

Sincerity had swirled through his baby blue eyes, and the guards I had up around me lowered a couple inches as the heady scent of his cologne penetrated my senses. He smelled like cloves and musk and something spicy. It was a combination I wanted to dive into and swim laps around.

"Aunt Merri," Levi called, bringing my mind back to the present. "We can't forget my wrestlers! We *have* to take them with us."

My little guy had a serious obsession with all things wrestling, and more than once, he'd nearly scared the life out of me by jumping off the back of the couch or something, just like he'd seen one of his favorite wrestlers do. Since my brother was always conveniently broke come the holidays or around Levi's birthday, I made sure to spoil my nephew as much as Warren would allow, buying him his favorite wrestling figures every year. They were his most prized possession.

"We won't forget your wrestlers, I promise."

"Do you think da-tek-iv Tristan likes wrestling?" he asked, butchering Tristan's title for at least the fifth time.

"*Detective*," I attempted again, stressing the word.

"That's what I said."

I gave up trying to get him to say the word correctly. "How about you just call him Mr. Tristan? I bet he'd be okay with that. And I'm not sure, little dude. You'll have to ask him."

We pulled up to the trailer Ozzy and Levi lived in a few minutes later, and my stomach sank like a boulder at the sight of it. The single-wide had never been in the best shape, but it seemed even worse than it had before I left town two months earlier. The skirting along the bottom was either missing or chewed through by large rodents. Rusted beer cans and empty liquor bottles lay strewn about the overgrown front yard. It looked like the crispy grass was in a losing battle with the weeds threatening to choke it out.

Beyond a set of rickety wooden steps and a front stoop with missing boards, the screen door swayed precariously in the breeze, only the bottom hinge keeping it from breaking off completely. Yellow police tape stretched across the doorframe, the sight of it twisting my stomach into knots.

This was no place for a child to live—hell, it wasn't fit for the rats that probably infested it—and I couldn't believe Ozzy had been okay leaving his son in a mess like this.

A piece of my heart broke off as I threw my car into park and turned off the ignition. It felt like swallowing glass when I forced down the tears trying to claw up my throat.

"My wrestlers!" Levi cheered, bouncing up and down in his booster. "Can I get out now, Aunt Merri?"

I checked the mirror to make sure Tristan was also parked and pushed my door open. "Yeah, sweetie. But stay on the path and wait for me." I didn't want him running through that calf-high grass and getting bitten by a snake or something. There wasn't a single place that was safe for a kid to play.

Levi made sure to stay on the path, skipping over the cracks like he was playing hopscotch as I rounded the back of my car, meeting Tristan there.

"I can't believe they were living like this," I said quietly, a knot forming in my throat and making my words come out in a croak.

I felt Tristan's gaze on the side of my face, but I couldn't tear my eyes from the dilapidated trailer that looked like it was going to crumble to the ground at any moment.

"It didn't look like this last time you saw it?"

I shook my head, an abrasive laugh breaking free. "It's always been a shithole, but it somehow got a million times worse since I left. The outline of the structure grew bleary as tears formed in my eyes. "And I left him to this. I just left him."

"This isn't your fault," Tristan said, his words coming out in a hard clip that had me twisting my neck to look up at him. "This is on his dad. You need to remember that while you work to give that boy the good he deserves."

His tone was so ardent, his features going from soft

to stone in an instant as he said them, that his words actually worked to loosen the muscles in my shoulders. It shouldn't be possible for a complete stranger to put me at ease, but there was something about Tristan Fanning that seemed to defy logic . . . at least for me.

I nodded, blinking rapidly to break the spell the swirling blue of his eyes pulled me into. God, he really was too handsome. If that were even a thing. His blond hair looked like it was a couple weeks past needing a cut, but somehow, instead of looking shaggy, it added to his appeal. Prominent, masculine brows sat over those beautiful eyes. His nose and cheekbones were sharp, but his square jaw evened everything out so he was still a hint more rugged than pretty. His button-down hugged wide, solid shoulders before tapering down to a lean waist, hiding what I was sure was a six pack, at the very least. He wore the shirt more casually than Warren did, open at the collar to reveal a hint of tanned skin at his throat, and, with his sleeves rolled up, putting a set of forearms roped with muscle on perfect display while his slacks covered strong, thick thighs.

Beneath the clean-cut trappings was something powerful, and while there was a little niggling in the back of my mind telling me I should be frightened, I couldn't stop going back to those eyes. It was the kindness in his blue eyes that put my fear at ease. Those eyes were likely to get me into trouble if I didn't watch myself.

If I wasn't careful, I could do something epically stupid, like develop a crush on this man, and that *could not* happen.

"It'll be a quick in and out," he said like he was trying to reassure me I could do this. "We'll head straight to Levi's room, get what he needs, then get the hell out of here. Sound like a plan?"

Before I could answer, Levi's voice rang out from the middle of the path. "Come on, you guys!" he said in exasperation. "You're goin' so slow, and I wanna meet the dog."

I curled my lips between my teeth and bit down to keep from laughing while a deep, raspy chuckle rattled from the chest of the man beside me.

Damn it, even his chuckle was attractive.

Giving Tristan a nod, I said, "Sounds like a great plan. Let's get this over with."

Chapter Six

Merritt

This time, as I wound my car through the streets of downtown Hope Valley and into a quiet residential area, Tristan was the one doing the leading.

The trip to the house I would never allow Levi to step foot into again had taken even less time than I'd anticipated. Turned out, my little guy hadn't had much . . . and most of what he had was barely a step up from trash.

A lot of his clothes were worn out, stained, or had too many holes and tears, and most everything else was too damn small. As it was, the pants he was currently wearing rode up higher on his ankles than they should have.

I didn't have much in the way of savings, but I'd take it all out if it meant getting Levi clothes that fit him properly.

He hadn't cared all that much about clothes and toiletries as we were gathering up his things. While Tristan and I went through to pack up the items a seven-year-old boy would need for everyday living and basic hygiene, my nephew had been stuffing his precious wrestling figures into his backpack. Problem was, he'd dumped out all his school work and supplies to make room for them.

It took a few minutes to convince him that school stuff *was* essential, no matter how much he might've hated math and science, but we finally got everything squared away and left that shitty trailer behind us.

Now we were on the other side of town, in a neighborhood where all the yards were freshly mowed and manicured and mature trees lined the roads, creating a tunnel-like effect with their branches and leaves. I spotted several people walking dogs and more jogging or powerwalking along the sidewalks, and a few raised a hand to wave as my car drove past them.

Seeing that reminded me of why I had once loved this town so much.

I'd grown up in the next county, a few towns over

from Hope Valley. It wasn't as nice, but we'd made the best of what we had and where we were. Being raised by a single mom with two kids meant things had been tight for us growing up. Mom had done her best. There was always a roof over our heads and food in our bellies, but there wasn't really anything left over for extras. We might not have lived in the best area, but it was certainly a hell of a lot better than where Ozzy had been living with Levi. I didn't want to think about how our mother was probably rolling over in her grave at what her son had become.

I'd barely been out of high school when my mother was diagnosed with cancer. It took her from us a few years later, but before she passed, she made me promise I'd take my share of the life insurance money and try to make the best possible life for myself.

Once she was gone, I'd done what I could to honor that wish by packing up my life in our small town and moving somewhere different, somewhere better. Hope Valley was the start of that amazing life. Then I met Warren and was convinced I was getting the life my mother had always dreamed of for me.

It had been a whirlwind relationship that, at the time, I thought to be a living fairy tale. Knowing what I now knew, I could look back on that time and see Warren wasn't trying to woo me like all those heroes in the romance books I loved to read, he was love-bombing the shit out of me, doing his best to convince me he was my knight in shining armor, when, all the while, he was molding me into the sweet, subservient woman he wanted me to be.

We were engaged before we even hit the one-year mark, and as soon as my big brother found out the man I was marrying had money, he packed up Levi and followed me to Hope Valley. At first I was excited to have him and my nephew close again. At least until I realized the only time Ozzy called me was when he needed money or a babysitter so he could go out and get loaded.

It wasn't long before the town I loved started to lose its luster for me, thanks to the two men in my life tarnishing it with their shadows.

But as we wound our way through Tristan's neighborhood, I was able to remember why I'd chosen this place. The shadows still remained, hanging ominously in the background, but I was determined to do everything in my power to fight them back this time.

The Suburban's turn signal flipped on, and Tristan finally pulled into the driveway of a pretty white two-story craftsman with a big bay window in the front and gorgeous stone accents.

"Looks like we're here, buddy," I told Levi, pulling

his attention away from the wrestling match happening in his lap between two of the figures he'd insisted he needed to hold during the ride over.

He crouched forward to get a better peek through the windshield. "It's pretty," he said. Then his eyes caught sight of something and widened with excitement. "He's got a basketball hoop!" His gaze darted to mine, the green glittering. "A dog *and* a basketball hoop? This place is *awesome*! Think Mr. Tristan will let me play?"

I smiled and lifted my shoulder in a shrug. "Only one way to find out."

He could barely contain himself long enough for me to round the car before he had his booster seat unbuckled and was standing, ready to launch himself out of the car as soon as I opened the door. And that was exactly what he did.

"Mr. Tristan! Mr. Tristan!" He raced up the driveway, moving so quick he struggled to stop himself before nearly plowing right into the man in question. "Can I play basketball on your hoop?" he asked on a shout, his arm extended and finger pointing at the hoop mounted at the side of the driveway.

My breathing stopped when Tristan reached down and ruffled Levi's hair while smiling at my nephew in a way that probably had ovaries exploding all across the county.

"Sure can, kid. I have a ball in the garage."

Levi started jumping in place. "Will you play with me?" He sucked in a gasp as a brilliant idea formed in his mind. "Can we play right now?"

I took a step toward them, ready to unlatch my little guy from his new favorite person. Levi was the freaking best, but he was a seven-year-old boy. They had more energy than a litter of puppies that had gotten into a case of energy drinks. "Oh honey, he probably can't—"

Tristan spoke up then and cut me off. "We can't play right now, 'cause we have to get you guys unloaded and all set up, right? But we can definitely play this evening after dinner. How's that sound?"

"Oh yeah! I forgot. I can help carry stuff in. I'm really strong. Just ask Aunt Merri." He twisted his little body at the waist to look back at me. "I'm a really good helper, right, Aunt Merri?"

I couldn't stop the smile from stretching across my face. "The very best helper, little dude."

Levi whipped back around to face Tristan. "See?"

I looked up at the man, and my lungs immediately stalled. The way Tristan was looking at me made my skin tight and my belly swoop. Those eyes were pinned to my smiling mouth, his own features softening in a way I definitely shouldn't find hot, but *damn it*, I did!

Tristan cleared his throat and blinked. As quickly as

the look was there, it was gone as he shifted his focus back to my nephew. Not once had he shown even a hint of aggravation or frustration at the way Levi seemed to latch onto him.

The same certainly couldn't have been said about Warren. We'd been together nearly the entire length of Levi's life, but once I'd seen the real man lurking beneath my husband's charming exterior, I did my best to keep Levi away from him. I didn't trust the man I married not to hurt him, so when Ozzy asked me to babysit, I did it at his place, spending the majority of those nights cleaning the trailer after putting Levi to bed. It hadn't always been as bad off as it was now, but my brother had never been one for housekeeping. Any other time I wanted to see my nephew, I took him somewhere fun, like the pizza place where he could play video games, or to the movies, or out for ice cream.

The one and only time I lowered my guard enough to bring Levi over for a visit, it'd been all the lesson I needed to ensure it never happened again. I thought it was safe because Warren was supposed to be at work. We'd been watching a movie in the living room and enjoying ice cream sundaes when Warren got home earlier than expected. He noticed Levi had accidentally gotten a drop of hot fudge on the couch and went ballistic, yelling and lecturing until my nephew began to cry.

He was only four at the time. I lost it at the sight of his tears. Something in me snapped, and I got in Warren's face, telling him he was never allowed to speak to Levi like that again. I'd paid for standing up to my husband later that night, once Levi was gone.

But Tristan didn't seem fazed in the slightest.

"What do you say I give you guys the tour, then you can get settled?"

I nodded, and with my hands on Levi's shoulders, we headed into the house. The first thing I heard as soon as he pushed the door open was the sound of nails skittering against the beautiful distressed hardwood floors.

A second later the dog came into view. Or at least I thought it was a dog. I did a double take, my chin jerking back in surprise. It was shaped like a pot roast, with an abnormally large bobble head and stubby little legs. It skip-walked the rest of the distance, letting out a sound with each step that was a cross between a wheeze and a grunt, mixed in with a little bit of a growl.

As soon as he reached us, he stopped and collapsed onto his side.

"Merritt, Levi, meet Doc," Tristan introduced. At the humor in his tone, I looked from the dog to him to find him watching the animal with affection carved into every plane of his face. Detective Tristan Fanning wasn't just a pet lover. He was a full-blown dog dad. And, damn it, but that was in my top three sexiest things about him so far.

"He's so cute," Levi shouted, dropping to his knees beside Doc.

"Is—is he okay?" I asked Tristan on a whisper. Doc wasn't moving, and I was beginning to worry that Levi might have his second traumatic experience in less than twenty-four hours.

Tristan waved his hand in the air. "Yeah, he's totally fine. That's his way of asking for a belly rub."

One corner of my mouth hooked up in a grin as I arched my brows. "*Asking*?" I stressed, my tone teasing.

Tristan's smile nearly knocked me on my ass. It was one thing to see it directed at someone else, but to be on the receiving end was something else entirely. "Okay, demanding is more accurate. He's a little spoiled."

At Levi's giggle, I turned back to find the dog had rolled the rest of the way onto his back, those short legs of his sticking straight up in the air. In that position, his jowls had fallen back, giving him a Joker smile, part adorable and part psychotic.

"He's like, the coolest dog ever, Mr. Tristan!"

I could have sworn I saw Tristan's chest puff out with pride as a flash of something that looked like victory flitted across his face. "Thanks, buddy." Then under his breath he added, "We'll see how Rhodes likes that."

"What was that?"

He blinked, giving a jolt like he hadn't realized he'd said that out loud. His grimace made him that much more endearing.

"Sorry. It's nothing, really . . . It's just, my nieces and nephew were all crazy about Doc until they met Rhodes's dog, Koda. They basically threw Doc over for her."

I curled my lips between my teeth to keep from laughing. "I take it that's a bit of a sore spot."

Tristan let out a derisive snort and crossed his arms as he watched Levi love all over his precious pet. "Just 'cause she's all purebred and regal and looks like she belongs in one of those dog food ads where she's running through a field somewhere doesn't make her better than Doc."

Holy crap. I didn't think it was possible for someone as handsome as Tristan to be adorable as well. "No, of course not," I said, trying my best to sound reassuring. "And Doc looks—" The word *regal* died on my tongue when I turned my attention back to the animal in question. He was currently thrashing his body from side to side to scratch his back on the floor, letting out a wheezy snort-grunt with each motion. "Well, he kind of looks like a ham. But a super cute ham," I added quickly. "And I don't know about you, but I'd take an adorable ham over some stuffy show dog any day of the week."

"Exactly!" Tristan said, that smile coming back in full force. And I realized that if I didn't build up a tolerance to this guy fast, I was going to be in serious trouble.

Chapter Seven

Merritt

I pulled a shirt out of my suitcase and shook the wrinkles out as best I could before sliding it onto the hanger and carrying it to the closet. The room Tristan had designated for me was really nice. I wasn't sure what to expect when it came to a guest room in the house of a single man who lived alone, but the large room with a decent-sized walk-in closet was a pleasant surprise.

The furniture was a nice, glossy white oak, the rustic style matching everything else in the house. There was a king-size bed with soft navy sheets, a matching bedside table, and a dresser. Like the rest of the house, there wasn't much in the way of decoration or personal touches. The furniture was all well-made and comfortable, and while his home was beautiful and cozy, I didn't see much of his personality in it. There were a few prints hanging on the walls here and there, and while they were pretty, they were all mass-produced landscapes and things of that nature.

The one thing I *did* notice was a top-of-the-line, fluffy dog bed in every common area in the house. Thinking back on that made me smile. It was clear the dog had a *very* comfortable life with Tristan, and I couldn't help but think that a man who was that sweet with his pet couldn't possibly be hiding a darker side beneath the surface.

But on the heels of that thought, I remembered that I'd let pretty words and looks fool me before. Tristan had been nothing but nice, but I couldn't afford to lower my guard, especially when I had Levi to think about.

With my last suitcase empty, I zipped it closed and carried it into the closet. When I stepped back out, the little black ball of fur was sitting inside the open doorway of my bedroom, his head tipped to the side as he stared up at me.

"Hi." Doc's head canted to the other side and he opened his mouth, his tongue lolling out the side. I crossed my arms and narrowed my eyes, "You know what, you are kinda cute." Doc panted and opened his mouth wide, and I swore it looked like he was smiling. I let out a chuckle. "Okay, fine. You're very cute. Happy now?"

He let out a little yip as if to say yes, he was.

"Oh, you're gonna be trouble, aren't you?"

He stood up and turned around, sauntering out of the room with his tail wagging like crazy.

"Aunt Merri," Levi called from his new room just down the hall from mine.

I popped my head in to find him posting his wrestling figures on the chest of drawers beneath his window while Doc snoozed on the floor a few feet away. Looked like the dog was already taken with my boy, not that I was surprised. "Yeah, sweetie?"

He turned from his task to look at me with a pitiful expression. "I'm *starvin'*," he stated. "I'm so hungry I could eat a whole cow all by myself."

I bugged my eyes out dramatically. "Wow. That's really hungry. That means I should probably feed you, huh?"

He nodded solemnly. "You should," he said with all the seriousness of someone much older.

I giggled as I moved into the room and pulled Levi into a tight embrace. Leaning down, I breathed in the scent of his shampoo and let it soothe me. After the day we both experienced, I had a feeling I was going to need a lot of these hugs before I felt completely settled. I reminded myself that my little guy was safe, and the people who had hurt us couldn't get to us where we were. But until that knowledge finally settled, I'd have to reassure myself by loving on my nephew until the tightness in my chest went away.

"Aunt Merri, you're squeezin' me to death," he croaked dramatically.

I forced myself to let him go, pulling back and ruffling his hair before finally letting my arms fall to my sides. "Well, we can't have that, can we? I'll go make you some dinner since you're so needy. You feel like anything in particular?"

He scrunched his lips to the side and tapped his chin, deep in thought. "Hmm. Oh! What about grilled cheese?"

I wasn't sure what Tristan had stocked, but he wanted grilled cheese, I'd go to the store and get the ingredients to make it happen. I arched a brow at him. "With tomato?" Levi had loved tomatoes since he was a baby, and the taste for them still hadn't faded.

He rolled his eyes. "Duh, Aunt Merri. That makes them the best."

"Of course. How could I forget."

I left him playing with his toys and headed down the

stairs. As I hit the landing to the first floor I noticed the discarded socks and running shoes that had been on the floor earlier were gone. As were the few dishes that had been sitting on the coffee table. Apparently Tristan had done a bit of cleaning. I started toward the kitchen when I heard his lowered voice. It sounded like he was talking on his phone. I decided to head back upstairs to give him some privacy, but as I turned to head back in that direction, I heard my name and pulled up short.

My mom taught me that eavesdropping was wrong, but I couldn't help myself. I inched closer to the kitchen.

"I'd really appreciate that, man." He paused like he was listening to the person on the other end of the call. "Yeah, I know. She really deserves to catch a break. I'm not askin' you to give her a job, just an interview."

My breath caught as I strained to hear better.

There was another pause on Tristan's end, then the deep timbre of his voice started up again. "That would be great. Thanks so much. I'll let her know." Another pause, followed by an exhale. "She's a good woman, and that kid is pretty awesome. I want to give them a fighting chance. They deserve some good, man."

I didn't have the first clue how to feel about what I overheard. My emotions were suddenly all over the place, swirling around inside me like a tornado. The one that stood out most, however, was appreciation. First, he offered to let us live here, and now he was calling around, trying to secure a job interview. That social worker had brought up both things in our meeting earlier, and it would have been a lie to say I hadn't been stressed. But in one day, this man had gone out of his way to help me clear both of those hurdles. And he barely knew me.

That guard slipped down a little further. It was becoming clearer with each passing hour that Tristan Fanning was a good man.

I heard him end the call and gave it a few seconds so it wasn't obvious I'd been listening in before I rounded the corner and entered the kitchen.

Tristan's head came up, his eyes colliding with mine. The blue flared right before he smiled gently. "Hey."

It felt like my heart was lodged in my throat. Not only because the man had shown me a kindness I hadn't experienced in too long without even knowing, but because, at some point, he'd changed out of his work clothes into something more casual. If I thought he looked good clean-cut, it was nothing compared to seeing him standing in his kitchen in his bare feet, wearing a simple pair of dark gray athletic joggers and a plain white T-shirt. "Hi." I cleared my throat and pointed toward the fridge. "Levi just told me he was hungry, so I was going to see about making dinner, if that's okay."

"Of course. You never need to ask. If you or Levi are hungry, never hesitate to help yourselves. I want you to feel like this is your place too. Nothing's off limits."

That guard slipped even further as a sincere smile pulled at my lips. "Thanks. I appreciate that."

He moved to the fridge and opened it for me. "I don't know what all you need, but I'm sure we have it. I asked Blythe to swing by the grocery store while we were packing Levi's things, and as you can see, she went a little crazy."

My head swiveled away from the contents of the stuffed-to-the-gills fridge and to Tristan. "You didn't need to do that."

He reached an arm up to rub the back of his neck, looking almost bashful as he admitted, "If you'd seen what was in here before, you wouldn't be sayin' that."

My smile grew wider. "Well, thank you. I appreciate you considering us like that."

When he turned his head, his gaze locking with mine, I realized how close the two of us were, standing in the opened door of the fridge, close enough for it to be dangerous. Despite the cold, the cloves and spice scent of his cologne wrapped around me and heated my blood.

Get it together, Merritt, the voice in my head chastised, snapping me out of the moment. I blinked and turned back to scan the contents of the fridge like they were the most interesting thing I'd ever seen.

I spotted the cheese and grabbed it, along with the small tub of butter. Then went for one of the large, plump beefsteak tomatoes in the crisper drawer.

"Is there, uh . . . is there anything I can help with?" Tristan asked, sounding like he might have been as unsure of himself as I felt in the moment.

"Um, sure." I tried to get my brain to cooperate on what I was doing and not on how good Tristan smelled. "Would you mind grabbing a loaf of bread? And I'll need a frying pan."

"Yeah, sure." He pointed to one of the lower cabinets. "Pan's in there," he directed, then opened the door to what I could see was a fully stocked pantry. "Uh . . . any preference on the bread? Looks like B got every kind the store carries."

I looked back over my shoulder and tilted to get a better look. Sure enough, the shelf was stuffed with several different types of bread. "Hmm. Let's go with the sourdough. And do you have a cutting board?"

He placed the loaf of bread on the counter beside me before moving away, only to return a moment later with a cutting board. "What's on the menu?"

"Levi's requested grilled cheese sandwiches." I

glanced his way and waggled my brows. "Because his seven-year-old palette is so sophisticated."

Tristan looked down at the selection I had before me, and his brows rose toward his hairline when he spotted the tomato. "Tomato for a grilled cheese? Not sure I've seen that before."

I smiled as I plucked it up and started cutting it into even slices. "Yeah, Levi loves tomatoes."

"Really?" Tristan asked with surprise.

I nodded. "Uh-huh. He actually used to eat them whole when he was a toddler. Would just bite into them like they were apples." The happy memory of my chubby-cheeked nephew sitting in his high chair with tomato juice and slime covering his face made me smile. "And as long as he's willing to eat them, you won't hear me complain. This way I can tell people he gets a full serving of his fruits *and* vegetables since most people can't agree on which category they fall under."

He chuckled, the huskiness resonating through the space. "Smart."

An idea hit me then a tiny way to pay him back for everything he'd done for Levi and me. "You know, they're actually really good. I'm already making sandwiches for Levi and me. It would be no problem to make a couple more if you're hungry."

He shot me a surprised look before his features softened. "Really?"

I swallowed, hoping the gulp wasn't audible. "Absolutely."

"That sounds fantastic. Thank you." He smiled, and I melted faster than the dollop of butter I'd just dropped into the pan.

Man, I was in so much trouble.

Chapter Eight

Merritt

Pulling the comforter up to Levi's neck, I sat on the edge of his bed and leaned down to brush the tip of my nose against his until he giggled sleepily.

"That tickles."

I pulled back, grinning down at the little boy who held my heart. "Did you remember to brush your teeth?" He nodded. "And did you go to the bathroom?"

"Yep."

"All right then. Looks like you're all set." I tucked the blankets around him exactly how he liked and stood from the bed, bending forward to press a kiss to his forehead. "I love you around the world and back again," I told him, using the same line I had every time I'd ever tucked him in.

"How many times?" he asked just like he always did.

I hummed thoughtfully before answering. "A hundred million."

"Well, I love you around the world and back again a *gazillion* times," he insisted, always having to beat me.

"That sure is a lot. Time to go to sleep and dream good dreams."

"Okay. 'Night, Aunt Merri."

"'Night, little dude," I returned, then started for the door. A night light in the corner provided a soft glow once I turned off the bedroom light. Before I could step out and pull the door closed, Levi called my name.

"Yeah, sweetie?"

"I really like it here."

My head squeezed and my nose began to sting. "I do too."

He chewed on his lip for a second before finding the courage to ask the question that was obviously on his mind. "Do you think, if we're really good, and do all our chores, that Mr. Tristan will let us stay?"

God, he was killing me. That little boy had been through so much in his short life already. He deserved some peace and security. He deserved not to worry or be scared, and in that very moment I made a silent vow to do everything in my power to make sure he got the childhood that had been stolen from him up to this point.

"I bet he'd let us stay a good long while." I moved back into the room and resumed my earlier spot on the side of the bed. "But, buddy, even if we don't stay here, I promise wherever we end up, it'll be great. We'll make it exactly how we want it."

"And it'll be you and me? I'll get to stay with you?"

There was no way to hide the fear in his voice as he asked that question, and I knew that had been weighing on him. "No matter what happens, it's you and me from here on out. I promise."

His little body relaxed, my answer chasing away whatever demons had been lingering and giving him the relief he needed. "Okay. Goodnight, Aunt Merri. Love you."

I forced down the emotion clogging my throat just then and won the battle against my tears. "Love you back, sweetie. More than you could possibly know. Now get some sleep."

He squirmed beneath the covers and rolled onto his side, settling in. I managed to hold it together until I made it into the hall and pulled the door closed. Then I rested my forehead against the cool wood and squeezed my eyes closed as sorrow and rage warred inside of me, battling for dominance.

"Everything okay?"

I started at the sound of Tristan's voice, jerking

upright and whipping around to face him. "Yes. No." I dragged a hand through my hair, the adrenaline I'd been riding all day long finally depleted, leaving me feeling worn down and exhausted. "I don't know," I finished on a weary sigh. "Right now it's taking everything in my power to keep from climbing into my car and driving to the hospital so I can beat the ever-loving shit out of my brother."

"Can't say I don't understand the desire. But instead of aggravated assault, how about I pour you a glass of wine?"

I heaved out a breath. "That actually sounds perfect."

He waved me away from Levi's door. "Come on. I'll crack open a bottle."

In the kitchen, he uncorked a bottle of red and poured me a glass before grabbing himself a beer from the fridge and popping the cap off. I sat on one of the stools at the island while Tristan stood across from me, and I sensed he was in detective mode.

I could feel his eyes on me as I took a healthy sip. "Feel better?" he asked before bringing the amber bottle to his lips and drinking a swig of his beer. Warren had always favored scotch, and now I couldn't stand the smell of the stuff. Just a whiff was enough to twist my stomach into knots.

The bottom of the glass clinked against the marble counter as I set it back down and swished the liquid around. "Not really," I answered honestly. "Maybe ask me again after a second glass."

He studied me closely, and I couldn't shake the feeling he was seeing more than most people would. "You want to talk about it?"

Bracing my elbows on the counter, I lowered my head and massaged at the ache in my temples. "Honestly, I'm not sure where to start. Do I start with my junkie brother who, despite having the world's greatest kid, couldn't give a shit?" I spat angrily. "Or should I start with the fact that I'm back in the same town as the man I married who got off on hitting me and belittling me every chance he had? Or what about the fact that I'm now responsible for the well-being of another human being—a human being that just so happens to be the most important person in my world? It felt like a dam had opened inside me, and now that it was all spilling out, there was no way to plug it back up.

"I can't let him get his hands on Levi again," I said, speaking of Ozzy. "I have to protect him no matter what, but when I think about what I look like on paper—what I looked like to that social worker today, I'm terrified they won't find me fit to keep him. I spent the past six years in an abusive marriage, so what does that say about my judgement? I'm technically homeless, jobless, and for the past two months, I've been on the run from my old life. I'm a disaster, and I'm afraid I'll never find my footing!"

Tristan rounded the island quickly. "Hey, hey. Stop that." He wrapped his fingers around my forearms and crouched down to put us at eye level. Somehow the touch of this man that I barely knew—despite the fact that I was now living with him—managed to ground me when I felt like I was spinning out. "Take a breath," he ordered.

I pulled in a deep breath, holding it for three counts before letting it out slowly.

"That's good. Just like that." He waited for me to take another breath before continuing. "Now, of course when you list it all out like that it's going to be overwhelming. But that's not how the world works. You have to take one step at a time, one *problem* at a time. Let's start with the easiest one first. You aren't homeless." I opened my mouth to argue, but he lifted a hand to stop me. "Look, I get that this all came out of nowhere, and I know we don't know each other well . . . *yet*, but this is your and Levi's home for as long as you want to stay. As for a job, I'm sure that won't be an issue for long."

"Thanks to you," I blurted before I could stop myself.

Tristan's brows snapped together in confusion. "What?"

"I heard you earlier," I confessed with a grimace. "I'm sorry. I didn't mean to eavesdrop." Well, that wasn't technically true, but he didn't need to know that. "I heard you on the phone with someone, talking about getting me an interview."

His throat worked on a swallow. "Listen, if I overstepped—"

Before I could think better of it, my hand shot out and came down on top of his, my fingers closing over his. His eyes darted down to where I was touching him, and I couldn't help but notice the way his throat worked on a swallow. "No, you didn't overstep," I insisted. "I'm beyond grateful for everything you're doing to help me and Levi. It's just . . . it's just that I don't understand why you're doing it. Why are you helping me?" I asked, finally putting to words the very thought that had been dogging every one of my steps all day long. "You don't know me. I could be a psychopath or planning to rob you blind."

He sucked in a deep inhale, the motion stretching the material of his shirt taut over his broad chest and revealing the outline of the muscles beneath a little better. "I'm not sure how to answer that."

My face pulled into a bemused frown. "What do you mean?"

"I don't know how to explain what's driving this need to help you, but it's been there from the very first time I saw you." My body went stiff as my mind reeled back to that day in Alpha Omega when everything had turned upside down. Tristan and Rhodes had been so focused on finding Blythe after she'd been taken by an asshole who'd been harboring a serious grudge; I hadn't realized he remembered me. "At the risk of scaring you off, I noticed you before I realized you needed help. But when you said your husband had been abusing you, this instinct sprang to life, and, well . . . I wanted to protect you."

There was so much to unpack with everything he'd just said, but all I could seem to focus on was he'd noticed me. Because I'd noticed him too, and it had scared the hell out of me.

"Look, I know we don't know each other, but Blythe cares about you, and if there's anyone's judgement I trust most in the world, it's hers. That's how I know you're a good person. And that's how I know that social worker is going to see the same thing. As for your husband, I'm going to do everything in my power to make sure you're safe, and he can't get to you."

I couldn't hold back my cringe at that word.

Husband. I hated that word now. That was another thing that needed to be taken care of. I'd looked into a divorce while I'd been in Baltimore, but being in a different state had complicated things. Now that I was back in Virginia, I felt this pressure pushing down on me to have that title stripped away from him. But that was a problem for a different day. Preferably when I wasn't hanging by a thread.

"I know you don't trust me," Tristan continued, his words bringing me back to the here and now, "and I totally understand that. I don't expect you to take what I say at face value. If anyone has the right to be guarded, it's you, and I'm not going to push that, but I want to help, Merritt." He sounded so earnest it made my chest constrict, my ribs squeezing painfully around my lungs. I looked into his eyes, searching that clear blue for deception, but there wasn't any to be found. "That's all. No ulterior motives. So . . . please. Just let me help."

I pulled my bottom lip between my teeth and bit down, pulling in a centering breath as I tried to get my heart to stop racing. Finally, I nodded. "Okay."

The relief at my agreement was written into every line and plane of his body. Then he gave me another one of those smiles that was like a wrecking ball to the wall I'd built to protect myself.

Chapter Nine

Tristan

I took in my surroundings as I lifted my pint and drank the icy cold lager, watching the Tap Room steadily fill with the after-work crowd. I wasn't sure there was ever a time when business was slow for Hope Valley's bar of choice. Even in the middle of the week.

As much as I liked the atmosphere of the place, I would have much rather been at home, answering the million and one questions Levi would have undoubtedly had and listening to him tell me about his day. To hear him tell it, he had an incredibly active and interesting life for a second grader. Probably had a more interesting life than most adults I knew.

But when Rhodes called earlier and asked if I wanted to meet for a beer, I'd forced myself to say yes, coming straight here from the station instead of heading home. It had only been a few days since Levi and Merritt moved in, and despite the step forward we'd taken together that first night, I could see that Merritt was still trying to find her footing in this new life she'd been thrust into.

I couldn't blame her. It hadn't even been a week. But if you asked me, she was taking it so much better than most people would have, which was a testament to how strong she was. So I decided to try and help ease the transition a little more by giving her some space. I didn't want to constantly be underfoot. I understood she and Levi needed their time together without me hovering in the background.

"Earth to Tris. Christ, man. You still with us?"

I blinked back into the present and took in the faces of my friends sitting around our table. Rhodes, Hardin, and Raylan were all watching me with different levels of curiosity and humor. "You say something?" I asked Hardin, since he'd been the one to speak and pull me out of my head.

He chuckled into the rocks glass as he brought it to his lips and sipped his whiskey. "You zoned out there for about two minutes. The lights were on, but no one was home."

I threw back the rest of my beer. I had a feeling I was

going to need more than one this evening. "Sorry about that."

Rhodes watched me from across the table, a shit-eating grin stretched across his face. "I'm willin' to bet my next paycheck he was spaced out, thinkin' about a certain woman."

I lifted my hand, shooting him the bird. I'd already known my future brother-in-law could be a pain in the ass at times, but since he found his forever with Blythe, he'd become downright insufferable. A happy Rhodes and a meddling, nosey, gossiping dickhead.

"It's nothing like that. I was just playing over my day in my head."

He snorted with laughter. "Did you forget I was there the first time you ever laid eyes on the woman? We were in the middle of a crisis, and you still managed to look like you'd gotten shot in the ass with Cupid's arrow."

That earned a round of laughter from the rest of the guys at our table.

My glare carried the promise of a future ass-kicking if he didn't stop giving me shit. "I don't know what you're talkin' about," I lied as heat crept up the back of my neck.

His brother Raylan joined in on the ribbing. "I don't know. Word on the street is you had her moved under your roof less than an hour after she hit town." He took a pull from his beer bottle. "Sounds sprung to me."

These assholes were right, at least partially. Not that I'd ever admit it to them. There was attraction there, had been since that very first moment. But whatever I was feeling went deeper than that. That protective instinct had settled right at the surface since Merritt got back into town, poised and ready to spring the instant anything threatened her. And as I got to know Levi better, that feeling also extended to him. It was like some basal, primal thing inside of me viewed them as mine to protect.

I let out a harsh exhale, ignoring the way my ribs were constricting around my lungs. "It's not like that. She needed help. She's been dealt a shit hand for way too long. I saw an opportunity to help her get on her feet, and I took it." It was the simplest explanation I could think to give them without having to dig deeper into everything else she made me feel.

"Besides, after all she's gone through, I'm sure the last thing on Merritt's mind is a relationship of any kind." I tried to tell myself those words didn't come out sounding as grumpy as they did in my head, but based on my friends' faces, I knew they had. "Jesus. I came here to have a couple beers and relax. Can we talk about somethin' else already?" I grumbled like a grumpy old man.

Just then, Lennix Paulson popped up, balancing a large round tray weighted down with drinks on one hand like the seasoned pro she was. Like her mother, Rory, this bar was in her blood, so when Rory finally retired from it, she'd handed it down to her daughter, just as her parents had done with her. Lennix's older brother, Zach, another one of my close friends, ran the family ranch, while Lennix kept the Tap Room afloat.

"Another round, fellas," she chirped, a bright smile curving up her painted red lips. She glided around the table, depositing glasses in front of each of us, having managed to get every one of our drinks correct without having to ask.

"You're a saint, Len," I grunted, grabbing my much-needed beer and sucking back a hearty gulp.

Her smile turned sassy as she shot me a wink. "What can I say? I live to serve," she teased. "You boys holler if you need anything," she said before tucking the tray under her arm and sauntering away.

Raylan shifted beside me, and I didn't miss the way his eyes trailed Lennix's every step as she moved farther away, winding through the crowd. The way he watched her piqued my curiosity, and my gaze bounced back and forth between them. I didn't miss the way the muscle in

Raylan's jaw strained when he spotted a man reaching for Lennix's arm to catch her attention. Or how his grip on his beer bottle tightened to the point it was a wonder it didn't shatter as she smiled up in a way that had the dude eating out of the palm of her hand.

And apparently I wasn't the only one who'd noticed.

Hardin let out a low whistle, his eyes widening. "Might want to watch yourself there, Ray. Zach catches you lookin' at his baby sister like that, he's liable to gouge your eyeballs out with a rusty spoon."

"Shut the hell up," Raylan groused, making the three of us laugh at his sudden surliness. "I'm not lookin' at her like anything. I just noticed the way that asshole grabbed her arm." His nostrils flared. "Who the fuck is that guy, anyway? He shouldn't be grabbin' on her like that."

I turned back in Lennix's direction. She was still smiling, and laughing now, as she reached out to caress the man's forearm. "I don't know, man. In my professional opinion, it looks like two people flirting with each other."

He shot me a killing scowl. "Yeah, well, he's too goddamn old for her. I mean, look at him."

Rhodes choked on his laughter. "He looks about your age, little brother. What's that difference? About twelve years?"

"Eleven," he answered quickly, like that number had

been sitting in his head for some time now. He seemed to realize he was still staring, looking for all the world like a man about to commit homicide, and shook himself out of his stupor. "Or somethin'. I'm not sure."

"Sure you aren't," Hardin snickered.

"Screw you, man. I'm not interested in her that way. She's like my little sister."

Hardin hooked a brow up, his expression reading, *whatever you say, you dirty, dirty liar.* But he was smart enough not to vocalize it, because something told me Ray wouldn't hesitate to take a swing at him just then. But in Raylan's defense, as much as I loved Hardin, sometimes his face looked exceptionally punchable.

Lennix's laugh carried over the din of bar noise, and all four of us looked over as she and the guy she was talking with pulled out their phones and started exchanging numbers.

Raylan's face suddenly grew red, and I began to worry I was going to have to lock my friend down to keep him from doing something epically stupid.

Ah hell. The man had it bad. And given that he was one of Zach's best friends, and had himself a bit of a reputation as a lover of the ladies, this could go bad very quickly.

He drained the last of his beer, slammed the bottle on the table, and pushed to his feet. Grabbing his wallet from his back pocket, he pulled out a few bills and tossed them onto the table. "I'm callin' it a night. See you assholes later."

With that, he took off toward the door.

Watching that situation play out was either going to be entertaining as hell or catastrophic. Hard to tell which way it would lean just yet. But I had a feeling it would go down in town lore—much like Hayes and Temperance's relationship had years ago—before it was all said and done.

"Shit," Rhodes grumbled into his drink. "I'm gonna have to kill Zach before he kills my little brother, aren't I?"

Hardin and I burst into laughter.

We hung around the bar for a while longer, listening intently as Harding regaled us with the most entertaining cases he'd had over the past couple weeks. As only one of two veterinarians in and around Hope Valley, Hardin was responsible for all kinds of animals, large and small. On any given day, he could spend his morning dealing with a tricky cow birth, then head back into the office to treat a sick bearded dragon.

Hardin threw back the last of his whiskey and knocked his knuckles against the table. "Well, guys, it's been a blast, but I'm outta here."

"You got the girls this week?" Rhodes asked,

speaking of Hardin's two daughters. He and his wife had gone through a nasty divorce late last year, and one of the main battles was over custody. She'd tried her hardest to screw him when it came to visitation, but in the end, he ended up with shared, now he gets his girls every other week.

"Nah, that's next week. I have an early morning appointment at a horse ranch over in Grapevine." He started moving backward, a grin tugging the corners of his mouth upward. "These were on you, right?" he said to Rhodes, pointing at his empty glass on the table.

Rhodes shook his head good-naturedly. "You really are an ass, man."

Hardin clapped him on the shoulder on his way past. "And you're a good friend. Catch you guys later."

A quick glance at my watch showed that two hours had passed. That was a decent amount of space, wasn't it?

Rhodes's chuckle pulled my attention to him. "Just go, man. It's obvious you're itchin' to get home. I got Blythe and the kids to get to anyway."

He didn't have to tell me twice. I threw down some money to cover my tab, shot him a quick "good night" and headed for the door.

Maybe if I drove fast enough, I could get home in

time to hear all about Levi's day before he had to go to bed.

Chapter Ten

Merritt

I wiped my sweaty palms on my skirt and breathed in for a three count, then let it out slowly as I stared through the windshield at the gorgeous, rustic structure before me. The glass and wood somehow blended perfectly with the mountainous backdrop, looking like it was meant to be a part of this land from the very beginning.

Although it really was beautiful, the size of Second Hope Lodge was intimidating, and what lay inside had my nerves tangling up my stomach. I hadn't even made it inside, yet I was already sweating in places that ratcheted up my discomfort ten-fold.

My cellphone buzzed in the cupholder in my center console, giving me a jolt. "Jesus, Merritt, get it together," I chided as I snatched my phone and clicked the button on the side to bring the screen to life. The text from Tristan that had just come through tugged the corners of my mouth upward.

Tristan: *Stop stressing out. You're gonna nail it. Bringing home pizza from Momma Gianna's for dinner to celebrate.*

My grin widened at his encouragement as my fingers typed out a reply.

Me: *Getting a little ahead of yourself, don't you think?*

I had officially been back in Hope Valley for a week and a half. Well, a week and three days, to be exact. And while the foundation of this new life I'd been thrust into was still a little wobbly, it was getting a little more comfortable—a little more solid—every day.

The home inspection with the woman from social services had gone better than I'd hoped, and with my brother currently locked up for child endangerment, I was looking into what it would take to gain full and permanent guardianship of Levi.

Tristan and I were still getting to know each other better, but I felt confident in saying that, while we weren't full-blown besties or anything, we were at least in the friendship area. He was easy to be around. I noticed that, unlike most people who wouldn't be able to ignore their instincts to push and prod, he waited with quiet patience for me to be ready. It was certainly unexpected, and I appreciated it more than he could possibly know.

Though he was careful with me, he was lively and loud and full of energy with Levi. He was more intuitive than anyone I'd ever met, knowing exactly how to handle each of us and spreading himself out in a way that made him accessible in any way Levi and I might need.

My phone buzzed with another text.

Tristan: *I have no doubts. Now get in there and show them how amazing you are.*

There was that intuitiveness at work again. He couldn't have possibly known how badly I needed a pep-talk in that moment, but he'd been there to give it.

With one last fortifying breath, I stuffed my phone into my purse and shoved out of my car. If I was impressed by the outside of the lodge, it was nothing compared to the beauty inside. Stepping into the lobby took my breath away. The Paulsons—the family who owned and operated the lodge, as well as the ranch it sat on—had managed to blend the perfect amount of rustic western and modern together in a way that totally worked. It felt like walking into John Dutton's living room on *Yellowstone*, complete with the cowhides on the floor and the oversized, butter leather furniture.

The woman at the front desk wore her silver hair in a fashionable bob. The lines around her smiling mouth and kind eyes told the story of a life full of happiness and laughter. The nametag pinned to her stylish blouse read *Becky*.

"Hey there," she greeted. "Welcome to Second Hope Lodge. What can I help you with, darlin'?"

I clenched my fists to hide the fact they were shaky. "Hi." The word came out too high-pitched and *way* too loud. I cleared my throat and tried again. "Hi. I'm Merritt Bell. I'm here for a one o'clock interview with a Ms. Young."

The woman's smile brightened. "Sure thing, dear. Why don't you have a seat? Make yourself comfortable, and she'll be right with you."

Her kindness helped to put me at ease. "Thanks so much."

"No problem. And for the record, you're gonna love workin' here. And I'm not just sayin' that because my family owns this place."

So Becky was a Paulson. Good to know. "Well, if that's the case, wish me luck with my interview."

She held up her hands and crossed her fingers for me.

"Merritt?" I heard a few minutes later, and spun

around to see a familiar face descending the grand staircase that led to the second floor.

My eyes widened and my mouth dropped open as I shot to standing. I recognized the woman from the obstetrician's office where I used to work. It had only been a few months since I last saw her, but with everything that had happened in that short time, it felt like a lifetime had passed. I moved in Ivy Young's direction, meeting her at the bottom of the stairs. "Oh, my gosh!"

She pulled me into a familiar hug, her rounded belly causing her to have to lean into the embrace so she could fully reach.

She pulled back from the embrace and smiled at me, "It's so good to see you."

The rest of my nerves melted away. "It's good to see you too. Wow. Look at you!"

She brought her hands to her stomach. "Yeah, I've kind of popped since I last saw you, huh?"

I let out a laugh. "You could say that." If my calculations were right, she was only around seven months or so, and I couldn't help but wonder how big the baby growing in her already was.

"Yeah, well, blame Connor," she grumbled, speaking of the father. "He failed to mention he was a huge-ass baby when he was born." Well, that explained it. "I'm trying not to think about how big this kid's head already is, because every time I do, I freak out."

I reached out and gave her arm a reassuring squeeze. "I'm sure everything is going to be fine. And just think, at the end of this, you'll get to hold your perfect little bundle in your arms. I doubt you'll even think about how much he or she weighs then."

"You're so right. But enough about that. Why don't we head upstairs and get this interview started? Though, now that I've put a face to the name, I'm confident it's only a formality at this point."

She shot me a quick wink before starting back up the stairs, and a rush of excitement filled my chest.

It took everything in me to maintain a modicum of professionalism as I walked out of the lodge and to my car. I barely managed to yank the door open and close myself inside before the excitement exploded out of me in an ear-piercing shriek.

I got the job.

I *got* the *job*!

Some people might have thought it was ridiculous to be

so excited over a job in housekeeping, where I'd be cleaning guest rooms and cabins, but I didn't care. I felt a sense of accomplishment I desperately want to share with someone.

I rummaged through my purse until I unearthed my phone and scrolled through my contacts until I got to the one I wanted. It rang twice before the person on the other end answered.

"Hey, honey. What's up?" Blythe greeted.

"Hey. What are you up to right now?"

"I was just about to start a load of laundry," she said, and I felt myself start to deflate before she added, "but if you have something better in mind, count me in. And I hate laundry so much, I'd consider a visit to my gynecologist better, so you won't have to work too hard to convince me."

I let out a laugh, my chest feeling lighter than it had in a really, *really* long time. I'd enjoyed my job at the doctor's office because it provided an escape from the nightmare I was stuck in at home. But a dark, ominous shadow always hung over my time there, reminding me that my escape was only temporary.

But this was different. There was nothing to escape from this time around. No cloud blocked out the light of what I'd achieved today.

"Well, I had a job interview today for a house-keeping position at Second Hope Lodge." She sucked in a breath, and I could practically feel the anticipation pouring off of her through the speaker. "And I got it!" I yelped.

Blythe let out a loud, whooping cheer. "Oh, my God. Merritt, that's incredible! I'm so happy for you."

Her excitement on my behalf made my eyes begin to sting, but I managed to keep the happy tears at bay. "Thanks." I chewed on my bottom lip as I battled a sudden wave of nerves in order to get out what I wanted to say next. "I was calling to see if maybe you wanted to meet for coffee to celebrate with me?"

"Are you kidding? Of course I would! I need to change out of my ratty house clothes. What do you say we meet at Muffin Top in about an hour?"

My smile was so big my cheeks started to ache. "That sounds wonderful."

Chapter Eleven

Merritt

The sun shone through the windows of Muffin Top, the coffee shop in town that served the best pastries and coffee, hands down.

Whether you were looking from something sweet or savory, flaky or dense, Muffin Top would have a pastry for you, and it was guaranteed to be one of the best things you'd ever tasted. It had been one of my favorite places since first moving to Hope Valley years ago, but early into my relationship with Warren, he started making little comments about how maybe I'd want to lay off the sugar and carbs because my clothes were starting to look a little tight.

Of course, he'd framed it in a way where he'd been looking out for my best interest. That care and concern started to get a little crueler the longer it took for him to get what he wanted, but instead of seeing the insults for what they were, he gaslit me into believing he was right to be upset with me for not listening to him, because he wanted me to be healthy so we could live a long, happy life together.

Muffin Top was one of the many things I lost in the years I was stuck in that marriage, and as I sat at the little bistro table by the window, drinking a perfectly sweetened cup of coffee and splitting a cranberry-orange scone *and* lemon-poppyseed muffin, I felt like I was taking back yet another piece of myself he had stripped away.

"You know, it's actually kind of kismet that you called when you did," Blythe said after taking a drink of her coffee. "I was actually about to reach out. I still have a few bins of clothes that Avett's outgrown. What I kept is still in great condition. Some of them still have tags on them. Tristan mentioned Levi could use some new duds, so I was going to call and see if you guys wanted to go through them and pick out anything he might want."

That warm feeling in my chest returned, only this time, it bloomed and began to spread, spanning out and traveling down my arms until the tips of my fingers began to tingle with it. And once again, I had to fight against the burn in the backs of my eyes. The sad fact was that I wasn't used to people being nice, and the Fanning siblings' kindness was like a one-two punch.

I still wasn't used to it. Each time I thought I might grow accustomed to Tristan's thoughtful gestures, he did something that floored me all over again. Even the jaded part of me that wanted to question whether or not all of his goodness was real was having trouble holding onto my doubts.

"Wow, Blythe. That's—" A knot formed in my throat that I had to fight to speak past. "That's so nice of you. I really appreciate it." Being able to afford new clothes that actually fit Levi was one of the things I'd been stressing about, and why I was so excited to get this new job. And, once again, thanks to Tristan, that was another item I was able to check off my list.

She waved me off like it was nothing. "Please, that's what friends do. They help each other out. I put the bins in the back of my car. We can move them to yours when we finish here." She popped a bite of muffin into her mouth, and a second later her eyes rolled back and she let out a groan. "Oh, my God. This muffin is the best thing I've ever eaten."

I let out a giggle and reached out to tear off my own bite. My eyes widened as the tangy-sweet flavor burst on my tongue. "Mm. That *is* good."

I took another bite, savoring the sugar and carbs in a silent *FU* to Warren.

A few seconds of silence passed between us as I enjoyed a piece of the scone. It wasn't as good as the muffin, but it was still delicious. While Blythe enjoyed her muffin, I took the opportunity to check my phone for messages. I'd texted Tristan to let him know how the interview went, wanting to share the good news with him, but so far, he hadn't responded. I knew he was probably busy, but I would have been lying if I claimed I wasn't eager to see what he had to say.

A tiny grin pulled at my mouth when I saw his reply was waiting for me, and it grew even bigger when I clicked on it and read.

Tristan: *I told you. In case you haven't noticed yet, I'm usually right. Pizza's on me. Text me a list of toppings you and Levi like.*

I pulled my bottom lip between my teeth as a bubbly, giddy feeling swooshed over me. Suddenly remembering that I wasn't alone, I exited out of the app and put my phone away. When I looked back up, Blythe was studying me closely from across the table.

"What is it?" I asked, reaching up to brush at my nose and cheek. "Do I have something on my face?"

Her expression gentled as she shook her head. "No. It's not that. You just look happy," she said softly as her mouth curled into a smile. And I could have sworn her eyes took on a glassy sheen. "It's really good to see you like this. To see you excited and optimistic. It's a great look on you, babe."

Crap, if she didn't stop soon I was going to start blubbering right here in the middle of my favorite coffee shop. "Please stop before you make me cry," I said on a laugh. "Because if that happens, I'll probably be too embarrassed to ever come back here. Then I'd have to make you suffer."

Her head fell back on a laugh. "All right, I'll stop." She reached across the table and placed her hand on top of mine. "I just wanted to say I'm happy for you. You deserve this."

"Thank you. I'll admit, it feels really good. I only hope it stays that way," I admitted, voicing the concern in the back of my mind since I'd returned.

Blythe's brows pinched in concern. "Have you seen him since you got back?" She didn't need to say his name for me to know who she meant.

I shook my head, staring down at the paper coffee cup in front of me and picking at the printed label stuck to the side with my nail. "No. But I know it's going to happen sooner or later in a town this size. I keep telling myself I'm prepared for it, but I'm not sure if that's true.

I mean, I haven't seen him since—" The words died on my tongue as I remembered back to that last beating. I still remembered how hopeless it all seemed, how he'd stripped me down until I felt like little more than a broken shell.

When I finally got away from him I wasn't sure I'd be able to put myself back together, but each day, I managed to slide a few of the jagged pieces back into place. I was terrified that one encounter and I'd be right back there again. I didn't quite trust myself yet to stand on my own two feet when it came to him.

Her fingers tightened around my hand in a silent show of support. "Well, first off, you don't have to face him alone. You have people who care about you, Merritt. You have a support system. Second, we need to see about getting you a divorce."

I heaved out a heavy sigh. "Believe me, I've thought about that. Filing without a lawyer is out of the question, because there's no way he'll agree to this. I've looked into hiring a divorce attorney, but the only ones I can afford are ones with lousy records. Warren's the one with all the money. If I can't come at him with someone who knows what they're doing, he'll drag this out as long as humanly possible. He's going to make the process difficult enough as it is, but if I go at him with a minnow instead of a shark, he'll do everything in his power to make my life miserable all over again."

Blythe's eyes sparked with fury on my behalf. It had been so long since I had a friend . . . a *true* friend who would have my back in any way . . . that I forgot what it felt like.

"Then we'll just have to find you a shark, won't we?"

I shook my head. "Blythe, I can't afford—"

She held up her hand to silence me. "Friends. Help. Friends," she stressed. And I'll keep saying this until it finally sinks in. Merritt, you are *not* alone. Okay?"

I sniffled, dangerously close to tears again. "Okay," I agreed on a husky whisper.

"We're going to do whatever needs to be done to sever every last tie to that son of a bitch."

We shifted the conversation to lighter things after that. She asked about how Levi was doing and shared about the changes that had taken place in her life in the time I'd been gone. She'd quit her job as a receptionist at the doctor's office where we first met, and started a small catering company, taking what she referred to as her stress cooking and using it for something productive. She was having a great time being her own boss and making a career out of something she loved.

She told me about how Rhodes proposed to her and shared some of the plans they'd made for the wedding so far. It was going to be small and intimate, just close friends and family, but from what she described, it was also going to be beautiful, and I'd been honored when she insisted I attend.

The conversation flowed so easily that it continued as we left the coffee shop and slowly strolled down the sidewalk toward where we parked. Downtown Hope Valley had always been a favorite of mine. It was full of charm and character. The buildings were a mixture of historic and new, all of them well-maintained. There was even a clock tower and a gazebo in the middle of town square where the town hosted things like outdoor movie nights and festivals.

As we passed by a small custom-furniture store, Blythe stopped to admire the dresser in the window display.

"Oh, look at that," she said in awe, moving closer to the glass. "That dresser is so pretty. I *have* to have that."

The piece she was looking at was pretty, but from where I stood, I could see the price tag attached, and it was enough to make my jaw drop. "It's nice, but it's crazy expensive. I could find you something beautiful at an estate sale for next to nothing and restore it for you way cheaper."

She swung her gaze my way. "You know how to do that?"

It was something I'd learned from my mother. When I was a kid, we'd hit up estate and garage sales on the weekends, hunting for treasures we could restore to their original glory or better. Some of my favorite memories of my mother were of us working for hours on pieces that others saw as junk. After she passed, it had been a sort of therapy for me, a way to feel close to her.

"I do. It used to be a hobby of mine." Warren wasn't a fan of anything that took my time and attention away from him. It was a wonder he'd even let me get the job at the doctor's office. "I'm a bit out of practice, but I could still make you something you'll love."

She let out a little squeak and bounced in place. "Deal! You let me know when you're free and we'll hit up some estate sales. It'll be fun."

A bud of excitement sprouted to life inside my chest and began to bloom. The thought of getting back to something that used to bring me so much joy took one of those jagged pieces and slid it back into place. "You're on."

"There you are!" a deep, familiar voice called out behind me, smothering the warmth that had been building inside me and turning my blood to ice. Warren was moving toward me at a fast clip, his expression a combination of concern and relief. A voice in my head was screaming to run, but every muscle in my body seized with fear at the sight of him, making it impossible to move. "God, baby, I've been going out of my mind. I haven't been able to think straight since I heard about your brother. I've been so worried about you. Thank God you're finally home."

Chapter Twelve

Merritt

Panic set in the instant he pulled me into an embrace. My lungs constricted so tightly no air could get in or out. Blackness started to creep in around the edges of my vision.

"I'm so happy you're safe. Now that you're back, we can go get Levi and move him in with us. I'll keep you safe. I'll keep both of you safe."

The mention of Levi broke through the panic that had been holding me in an iron grip. The underlying threat hidden beneath the shiny veneer of a loving, adoring husband and uncle. I would die before I let him anywhere near Levi.

My fight or flight instinct finally kicked in, and I began to thrash in his hold. "Let go of me!" I shouted, shoving at his arms until I broke free and stumbled back.

Blythe was there in an instant, wrapping her arms around me to hold me steady.

He actually had the audacity to look shocked, and slightly wounded, at my outburst. "Merritt, sweetheart—"

He took a step toward me, but Blythe moved fast, shifting me to the side and stepping in front of me. "Don't you touch her!" she barked, the rage in her voice drawing several of the people around us up short. We were attracting an audience, but in that moment, I couldn't find it in me to care. I was too busy trying to keep my knees from giving out as my body started to tremble uncontrollably. "You stay the hell away from her," Blythe continued.

Warren's head jerked back at the venom flying in his direction, but I had to hand it to him, the man was the best actor I'd ever seen. He deserved an Oscar for how well he played the role of a bewildered, worried husband.

"What in the world is going on? I'm just trying to talk to my wife." He shifted his attention over Blythe's shoulder. "Baby, I've missed you so much."

"You don't get to talk to her. You shouldn't even have the right to look at her or breathe in her direction. You need to turn around and walk away."

"Look, I don't know what this is all about, but this is

between me and my wife. It has nothing to do with you." The clench in Warren's jaw and flash in his eyes was one I recognized well, and seeing it directed toward my friend made me fear for her safety.

"Blythe." I grabbed hold of her arm and tried to tug her back, to get her the hell away from the monster she was standing up to, before something unthinkable happened. I didn't know what I would do if Warren hurt her because of me. "Please," I begged quietly, not sure exactly what I was pleading for. For her to stop? For her to walk away? To forget about me and protect herself?

Blythe snorted derisively, her glare intensifying by the second. "You know, you might think this adoring husband act is working for you, but I know the truth," she said threateningly. "I know it's all bullshit. And I know the monster you are beneath this façade." She waved her hand in front of him.

That tick in his jaw became more pronounced, and I knew he was struggling to keep the hidden dark side of him—the *real* him—from breaking free in the face of Blythe's dressing-down.

"Look, I don't know what she's told you, but my wife is confused. She's been under so much stress lately, and she's never been one to handle pressure well. It's my job to take care of her. I'm the only one who can help when her mind starts playing tricks on her."

My skin grew clammy as fear washed over me. This was what he did, what he was so brilliant at. Convincing people to come around to his way of thinking was a skill he'd fined-tuned and used regularly, and the thought that the only real friend I've had in years might actually believe him twisted my stomach as bile clawed its way up my throat.

However, as it turned out, I was scared for nothing.

"I know what I saw," she threw back, the anger practically vibrating off her and causing the air around us to shimmer. She stepped closer, her tone full of menace. "And I know she didn't do that to herself."

Warren stiffened. "I don't know what you're accusing me of, but I'd be very careful if I were you," he said on a low growl.

She wasn't deterred in the slightest. "And I also know a narcissistic, manipulative, gaslighting piece of shit when I see one."

Oh God.

"Now, if you don't turn around and walk away right now, I'm calling the police."

She'd called his bluff, and Warren knew it. But I didn't think for a second he'd just give up. He'd take time to regroup and strategize, all while coming up with a punishment. That was how his twisted brain worked.

He turned his attention back to me, his mask in

place once again. "You're clearly upset, and that's the last thing I want. I'll go for now, baby. Just know that, when you're ready to come back, I'll be waiting."

With that, he turned on the heel of his loafer and started back in the direction he'd come from. At the sight of his retreating form, my body gave out, and I would have fallen to my knees if it weren't for Blythe holding me up. As it was, my heart was beating so fast it was a frantic flutter in my chest that I could feel through my skin.

"We need to go," Blythe informed me as she started tugging me down the sidewalk toward her car.

"Go where?"

Her eyes met mine, and her arm around my waist banded tighter, like she was trying to pour all her strength into me, knowing I needed it. "We're going to the police. We're going to make sure that asshole can't get anywhere near you or Levi ever again."

TRISTAN

• • •

Harrison's desk chair let out a high-pitched whine of protest when my partner flopped onto it aggressively, the expression on his face thunderous to go with the tense lines of his body.

He blew out a frustrated huff as I shoved the white paper coffee cup I'd picked up for him from Muffin Top onto his desk.

"Thanks," he grunted, lifting it to his lips and taking a sip.

"I take it you didn't have any luck?" While I'd been working our drug case from this end, trying to find some sort of connection between the overdoses, Harrison had gone to the prison to try and get Oswald Garrison to tell us where he got it. More than once I'd questioned how Merritt and Levi could be related to a man like him. Oswald—or Ozzy, as he was commonly referred to—was a blight of society. A waste of oxygen. He couldn't have been more different from the rest of his family if he tried. On top of being a worthless junkie, the guy was also a raging asshole. I'd gotten word that he'd been in two fights already because the prick didn't know when to shut his mouth.

I would admit, my curiosity had been piqued, and I'd come close to asking Merritt about her older brother more than once, but I always managed to stop myself. She hadn't brought him up on her own, and I certainly didn't want to pry and risk making her uncomfortable. I managed to come to terms with the fact that she'd tell me in her own time . . . or not at all. It was her choice.

Harrison cut his eyes at me. "You kidding? I couldn't even get in to see him. Asshole got himself shanked by mouthin' off to another inmate who's a hell of a lot further up on the totem pole than our boy—not that he seems to care. He was laid up in the infirmary, bitchin' and moanin' about needing pain meds, which they won't give him since he's an addict. Refused to say a word unless I got them to dose him with something."

"And I'm guessin' you didn't."

Harrison let out a snort and rolled his eyes, rocking his chair back and kicking his feet up on his desk as he took another hit of coffee. "You kidding? I wouldn't have helped him get a fix even if he hadn't been a pain in the ass this whole time. But considering he has been, I got a fair bit of enjoyment refusing and watching him suffer."

I let out a chuckle and rocked back in my seat, twirling the pen I'd been holding between my fingers. "I just don't get it," I started a few seconds later. "Garrison is nothin' like the other OD's. They don't run in the same circles, share the same lifestyles. Hell, I don't think he even crossed paths with any of them."

All the other people who'd overdosed on the same cocktail as Merritt's brother were in a different league.

They were the types to golf every weekend and have memberships at an exclusive country club. Most of them were from well-off families and had connections in local politics.

"He's not someone they'd even want to share air with. So how'd he get his hands on a batch of heroine that exclusive?"

"Your guess is as good as mine. We've been digging nearly a week and a half and can't find a single connection anywhere. I hate to say this, but unless that shit stain gives up his supplier, I'm afraid we've hit another dead end."

I had a sinking feeling he was right. On that thought, my desk phone rang, the display showing that the call was coming from the front desk.

I plucked it up and brought it to my ear. "Fanning."

"Detective," Officer Michaels, the patrolman currently working the front, greeted, "You've got a visitor."

I pushed out a huff. "Swear to Christ, if it's Sue Ellen Mayfield again—"

"It's your sister. And she's got someone else with her. Says she needs to see you right away."

A chill passed down my spine. Blythe didn't just show up unannounced, and from the tone of Michaels's voice, something serious was going down. "Send her back," I said in a rush, then slammed the phone onto its cradle and shot to my feet.

I was vaguely aware of Harrison following after me as I started winding my way through the maze of desks that made up the bullpen.

"What's going on?" he asked, his legs moving fast to keep up with my pace.

"My sister's here. She—" Before I could finish my sentence I spotted Blythe coming off the short set of stairs with a worried look on her face. But as quickly as I recognized that, my attention was stolen by the woman she was holding onto.

Merritt was pressed into her side, her shoulders hunched like she was trying to curl in on herself and disappear.

I stopped a few feet in front of them, taking a quick second to get myself together and rein in the wide range of emotions suddenly churning inside of me like a squall. "What the hell happened?" I directed the question to Blythe after a quick glance showed Merritt's pale green eyes had a haze to them like she had closed herself off.

Her unease was quickly replaced by a look of anger so terrifying it would have every man in the vicinity cupping their balls for protection.

"It was *him*," she said. And just like that, a blanket of red coated my vision.

Chapter Thirteen

Tristan

It was taking everything in my power to keep from losing my shit, and with each passing second, the grip on my control slipped just a little more. The only thing keeping me in check was the realization that an outburst from me was the last thing Merritt needed.

We'd moved to a conference room for more privacy, and Harrison had taken Merritt's and Blythe's statements when it became obvious I wasn't going to be able to. It was hard enough listening to them recount what had happened, how he'd tried to manipulate the situation with my sister and insinuated that Merritt wasn't mentally sound.

I'd seen that behavior before. It was right out of the abuser's handbook. As a cop, I'd dealt with my fair share of domestic situations. But this was the first time one had touched me so closely, and I wanted to find that prick and rip his spleen out.

Merritt had been working so hard to pick herself up and start over after finally getting away from him. With every day that passed, I saw a little more light in her eyes, a little more curve in her smile. She seemed happy, and she'd been so damn excited about getting that job. This should have been a day of celebration, and that asshole popped his head out and managed to ruin it for her.

The light that had been steadily getting brighter dulled once more. Where she'd been holding her shoulders straight and her head high, now she hunched over like she was trying to hide herself in plain sight. Her cheeks had lost their rosy glow, but what was worse than all of that was she was back to clenching her hands into fists. I'd seen her do that off and on whenever she got anxious, and more than once I'd spotted blood where she'd squeezed so tight her nails had broken the skin on the heels of her palms. That was how she was holding them right then, and the thought that she might be hurting herself made my stomach sour.

I wasn't able to stay quiet any longer after seeing that. Leaning forward in my chair, I rested my forearms on the table and met her gaze. "Merritt, I think you need to file a temporary restraining order."

Her eyes flashed with panic as her head whipped around in my direction. "No. No restraining order. That'll only make things worse. He cares too much about public perception. After what happened today, he'll probably back off. He can't stand the idea of being embarrassed. He won't want to go through that again."

I could read her like a book, and I knew she was trying desperately to convince everyone in the room that was the most likely outcome. But she knew better.

I lowered my voice, reaching over to place my hand on hers. I slid my thumb between her fingers and her palm and gently coaxed her fingers to loosen. I let out a sigh of relief when she unclenched her fists, and I didn't miss the way my sister watched the exchange, missing nothing. "Honey, you don't really believe that, do you?"

She sniffled, those sage-green eyes going glassy as her lower lip began to tremble. I could see her fighting to keep tears from falling and applauded her strength when she succeeded. "No," she admitted quietly.

"You know I'm not gonna let anything happen to you and Levi, not as long as you're under my roof. But this is another layer of protection."

"But it'll make him so mad."

"He can get as mad as he wants. He still won't be allowed to get anywhere near you. And if he does, I'll haul his ass to jail myself."

"He's right, honey," Blythe spoke up. "I know you're scared, but I really think you should do this. It'll make a statement. Right now he thinks he can still manipulate you. This'll show him how wrong he is. Don't let him take more from you than he already has. You're on your way to a great life; he doesn't get to ruin that."

I really had lucked out in the sibling department. Between my two step-siblings, my younger half-brother, and Blythe, I had it better than most. But it was situations like this that reminded me of how big a badass my big sister was. She took shit from no one and wouldn't hesitate to go to bat for the people she cared about. It put me at ease that she'd clearly brought Merritt into that circle. She deserved a friend as fierce and loyal as Blythe.

"Okay," Merritt finally said after giving it some thought.

My shoulders sagged with relief. I was going to do everything I could to make sure a judge granted her that TRO. I'd even include the pictures Rhodes had taken of that final assault as evidence to show exactly the kind of man Warren Bell was.

He wasn't going to get away with hurting her. And I was going to make sure he never had another opportunity to scare her and force her back into that shell she'd worked so hard to climb out of.

"You're making the right decision," Harrison assured her.

She slowly straightened her spine, lifting her chin so she was no longer hiding. She was still shaken up after what had happened, but as we all sat there, I could see her fighting to find the version of herself that had come out of the shadows these past few months. Warren had seriously underestimated Merritt's strength and courage.

It was a relief to see it hadn't taken her long to find that backbone. I already knew it had been there all along. It just took her a second to realize that herself.

*M*ERRITT

D*espite my insistence* that I was fine and more than capable of taking care of myself, Tristan had insisted on cutting out of work early and driving me home, despite the fact I had driven myself into town earlier.

"Don't worry. I'll take care of it," was all he'd said when I mentioned that my car was still parked downtown, a couple blocks from Muffin Top, and it took me by surprise that my immediate reaction was to trust him.

As I sat in the passenger seat of his suburban, surrounded by the scent of cloves and spice that was so distinctly Tristan, I realized I trusted him with more than my car. That was why I'd agreed to the restraining order in the end. Because if he thought filing one was for the best, I trusted that he was right.

"What's goin' through your head over there, Dandelion?"

My head whipped around in his direction, my brows pinching in curiosity. That was the first time he'd ever called me that. "Dandelion?" I questioned, unsure what the nickname symbolized. "Like the *weed*?" My top lip curled up.

His chuckle filled the cab of the car. "I can see by the look on your face you think that was an insult, but did you know the dandelion is actually a symbol of resilience?"

My chest stuttered as the meaning of what he said sank in, leaving me momentarily speechless. "What?"

Tristan glanced my way for a brief moment before looking out the windshield and explaining. "Dandelions represent hope, healing, and resilience. Most people might look at one and see a weed that needs to be pulled out. But I see this small, delicate thing that looks like it should be fragile, but is actually so much stronger than it's given credit for." He lifted a shoulder in a shrug, unaware that his words had taken root inside me and were spreading, filling spaces that I hadn't realized were empty.

"When I look at you, I see all those things, so it seems like a fitting nickname, if you ask me."

The car fell into silence as I tried to sift through all the emotions stirring around inside me and picked out the strongest one. Gratitude. That was the one that stood out most. I was grateful to Tristan and everything he'd done for me. I was grateful he believed I had that in me. And I was grateful he was helping me to believe it as well.

"You asked what was going through my head a second ago."

He cast a curious glance my way and nodded. "I did."

"Well, I was thinking I'm beginning to trust you more than I've trusted anyone in a very long time."

His chest rose on a sharp breath, and I didn't miss the way his fingers flexed around the steering wheel. "Christ, Merritt," he ground out, his voice going low and raspy. "Can't begin to tell you what a gift it is to hear that from you."

A smile tugged at my lips as I sat back in my seat and took in all the beauty of Hope Valley as it passed by. A minute later, Tristan took a turn that would lead us in the opposite direction of his house.

"Where are we going?"

He tapped the clock on the dashboard. "Schools about to let out. We gotta pick up the little man."

I sucked in a sharp gasp, my eyes going wide. So much had already happened today that I'd completely lost track of time. But leave it to Tristan to be on top of things. I was beginning to see he wasn't just trustworthy, he was dependable too.

"Shit," I hissed. "The booster's back in my car. I totally spaced on grabbing it."

"Don't worry about that. I've got it covered," he said, throwing a thumb over his shoulder.

I twisted around and spotted a brand new, stain-free booster seat on the back bench on the passenger side.

"You bought your own booster?" I asked in astonishment. "When? Why?"

"Day after you guys moved in," he answered casually, like it was nothing, when in reality, that small act of thoughtfulness was *everything*. "Thought it would be smart to be prepared in case you ever needed me to pick Levi up for you or somethin'. Speaking of . . . we should probably add my name to the pick-up list for the school. Now that you have that job, I'm sure I'll need to carry some of the load."

I sniffled, that burn in my eyes returning in the face of all Tristan's kindness. "You better stop being sweet or you're going to make me cry."

He let out a laugh that made my belly fizzy and warm like I'd just swallowed a bottle of champagne. "We wouldn't want that."

"No, we wouldn't," I said with mock grumpiness. "Because I'm a seriously ugly crier."

He guided the Suburban into the parking lot and joined the line of cars waiting for school to end. "I seriously doubt you could look ugly doing anything."

I let out a snort and crossed my arms over my chest. "You have no idea. There's snot and blotches and swollen noses. It's a whole thing."

"Well it would be a shame for you to have to walk into Momma Gianna's blotchy and snotty and swollen."

"Momma Gianna's?"

He shifted into park and twisted in his seat to face me. "Yeah, Dandelion. I told you, we're celebrating your new job tonight."

"Oh," I breathed, that fizzy warmth growing more intense by the second. "I didn't realize we were still doing that."

He reached out then, the pads of his fingers brushing against my temple and sending a tremor through my body as he tucked a strand of hair behind my ear. "Of course we are. Something great happened to you today, and there's no way that piece of shit is going to tarnish it for you. From here on out, the three of us are celebrating the good because it's the very least you guys deserve. And it's about damn time you and that little guy start getting what you deserve."

My guard was so low I was beginning to wonder if there was any point in keeping it up any longer. Because something told me it never stood a chance against Tristan Fanning.

Chapter Fourteen

Merritt

I looked up from the stove as Tristan came walking into the kitchen, dressed in his sweats and tee with Doc cradled in his arms like a baby. The dog's stubby little legs were shooting straight up in the air as Tristan casually rubbed his belly, and I had to roll my teeth between my lips to keep from laughing. Levi and I had been living with Tristan for a little over two weeks now, and it had become clear that, if Tristan was home, the dog didn't do much walking on his own. It was adorable and ridiculous at the same time.

It was also more than a little problematic. Doc wasn't exactly light, so every time Tristan carried him around, the muscles in his biceps and forearms flexed and were on full display.

I hadn't been able to stop thinking about all those bombs he'd dropped on me last week. The booster seat and the nickname, not to mention all the other sweet, meaningful things he'd done between then and now without even realizing; it was starting to get to me.

From where I stood, the man was the total package. Handsome, kind, funny, loved animals and kids, and selfless. I kept searching for a flaw, for any sign that there might be something darker lurking beneath the surface, but I was coming up empty. He was a good man. A *great* man. And that knowledge scared the hell out of me, because it made it impossible not to like him.

"Something smells great," he said as he continued with Doc's belly rubs. "Whatcha cookin'?"

"*Chicken stir fry*," Levi answered in a tone that would make you think I was feeding the kid dirty mop water.

I twisted from the stove to where he was sitting at the island, drawing pictures on pieces of construction paper. I propped a hand on my hip as I shot him a look. "Whoa. What's with the tone, little dude?"

His face scrunched up like he'd just caught a whiff of Doc's poop. "It's got vegetables in it." He said *vegetables* like the word personally offended him.

My brows climbed up my forehead. "What's wrong with vegetables?"

"They're disgustin'," he stated with a straight face. "And you put them in *everything*. Even the macaroni and cheese you made had broccoli in it. You're puttin' so much green in stuff my skin's gonna turn green!"

I shot Tristan a glare, silently warning him to keep his trap shut when he snorted.

"I'll have you know that vegetables are good for you." And I had a feeling they hadn't exactly been a staple of his diet up until recently. "They help you grow big and strong and keep you healthy."

"And they taste like dirt," he deadpanned.

"They do not," I declared in offense. "I make them taste good. And that broccoli was drowning in so much cheese it was barely healthy."

He threw his arms up exasperatedly. "Then why even put it in?"

"He's got you there, Dandelion," Tristan added unhelpfully.

If he wasn't careful, I was going to slip something into his food that would have him running to the bathroom every five minutes.

I gave Levi a stern expression and pursed my lips. "Well, I'm the adult and I make the rules, and one of my rules is you'll eat vegetables at least once a day. End of discussion."

I wouldn't ever admit it to either of them, but I might

have been going a little overboard with the vegetables. But I knew Ozzy hadn't cared enough to make sure his son was eating healthy, balanced meals every day. There was also a small, irrational part of me that was willing to do anything to make me look good to Levi's case worker. If vegetables were the deciding factor in whether or not the state would grant me custody of my nephew, I'd grind them up and mix them into a freaking cake.

He crossed his arms over his little chest and stared me down, a challenge glinting in his eyes. "Fine, but I get ice cream after dinner."

I mimicked his stance. "Are you trying to haggle with me right now?"

"I don't know what that means."

Sometimes I could swear the kid was too damn smart for his own good. "How about this, you keep giving me grief and I'll throw out all the ice cream in the house and replace it with nonfat frozen yogurt."

"For the love of God, kid, back down," Tristan muttered out of the corner of his mouth.

Levi blew out a loud, obnoxious raspberry, but didn't say another word.

I grinned victoriously and turned back to give the food a stir. "Now go put your stuff up. Dinner's about ready."

"Yes ma'am." He hopped off the stool, gathered up his paper and crayons, and bolted out of the kitchen.

Doc let out a bark and began to squirm in Tristan's arms, demanding to be put down so he could chase after his boy.

We watched them disappear around the corner, and once they were gone, I turned back to Tristan with a look on my face my mom used to give me and my brother when we in trouble for something.

Tristan held his hands up in surrender, a cheeky grin on his face that looked so good it was difficult to maintain my frustration. "I'll eat all my veggies, I swear. Please don't make me eat nonfat frozen yogurt.

The smile I'd been battling broke free. He was impossible to stay mad at.

I STEPPED out into the hall and tugged Levi's bedroom door partially closed. A quick peek through the crack showed his chest was rising and falling in a deep, steady rhythm. He was already out like a light. I guess eating his vegetables had really taken it out of him.

A small grin pulled at my lips as I gave myself

another few seconds to simply stand there and watch him. I hadn't known a human being had the capacity to love so big, so profoundly, until Levi came into this world.

I'd always wanted kids of my own. A part of me still did. And I knew the love I'd have for my own children would be the same as what I felt for the little boy curled up beneath his wrestling sheets, because as far as I was concerned, Levi was mine in every single way that mattered. It was something I'd always known, but these last few weeks had cemented that feeling.

I had to find a way to make this permanent. I was prepared to fight for that, because it was the right thing to do, but I still hold out hope I could convince Ozzy to do what was in Levi's best interest and give me custody. I just had to find the courage to go see him to ask.

I shook myself out of those morose thoughts and headed downstairs to clean up the mess from dinner. Only, I entered the kitchen to discover Tristan had already done it while I was upstairs getting Levi ready for bed.

The small kitchen table where the three of us ate dinner together every night was cleared. The dishes were loaded into the dishwasher. The stovetop and counters were wiped clean. And there was a newly-poured glass of red wine sitting on the island beside an opened beer bottle.

"Wow. Tristan, you didn't have to do all of this."

He looked over his shoulder at me from where he stood at the sink, drying off the skillet that always needed to be washed by hand because it was too big for the dishwasher. "Of course I did, Dandelion." Every time he used that nickname, it sent a shiver through my body. "You did all the cookin'. It's only fair I clean up the mess. That was always the rule in our house when I was growing up."

I smiled and reached for the wineglass, bringing it to my lips and letting out a pleased hum at the flavor. It hadn't taken Tristan long to discover which wines I favored, and like his beer, he kept the house stocked.

It was one of the many little things we'd gotten to know about each other over the past few weeks. I learned he wasn't a fan of chocolate itself, but loved chocolate cake. He passed out less than halfway through a marathon race to raise money for Hope House because he'd gotten cocky and was convinced he could do it, even though he'd never run that kind of a distance and didn't train for it. I learned he liked bacon as a breakfast food, but not on burgers, and he was scared of the dark until he was ten.

In return, he learned I loved mushrooms, hated red velvet cake, and I broke my arms twice in fifth grade.

"I've heard some stories from Blythe. Your parents seem pretty great."

Tristan gave a small grin as he returned the skillet to its cabinet and turned to face me, leaning his hips back against the counter and picking up his beer. "They are. My mom was always the cool one to all my friends when I was growin' up. Mostly because she baked a ton and handed it out to anyone who ever came over to the house. And Trick was a badass. I'll admit, havin' a cop in the house put a bit of a damper on my teenage rebellion, but he was never too harsh. He had a way of talkin' to me whenever I screwed up that made me really think, you know? Made me respect him. He's the reason I wanted to become a cop. One of the best days of my life was when he and my mom got married."

My brow furrowed. "Oh, so Trick is your stepdad?" I didn't know that.

Tristan nodded, taking a swallow of his beer. "Yep. Started dating my mom when I was twelve. They got married not long after. But to me, he's my dad. It's the same for Blythe."

I had a million questions, but refrained from asking because I didn't think it was my place. However, my curiosity must have been written all over my face because after another sip of beer, he said, "You can ask. It's all right."

The question fell right out of my mouth. "Is your biological dad out of the picture?"

Tristan snorted, and although he was still smirking, this one had a bitterness to it. "In a profound way."

My head tilted to the side. "What do you mean?"

"He's in prison."

My back shot straight and my wineglass froze midair. "Tristan," I said quietly, my heart squeezing painfully. "I'm sorry. You don't have to talk about this if—"

He pushed off the counter and moved to the island, bending at the waist to rest his forearms on the surface. He twisted the beer bottle between his hands. "No, it's okay. It used to be really hard to talk about, but not so much anymore. Therapy helped, so did talking to my mom and Trick." He pulled in a breath as though he was bracing himself, then dove in. "My biological father was an addict, just like Ozzy. Only, he took it a step further and started dealing in order to support his habit. Problem with that was, he couldn't stop dippin' into the product he was supposed to be sellin', and didn't have the money to cover the cost of what he stole, so the guy he worked for decided that taking me and Blythe might light a fire under him to pay up."

I rounded the island before I realized I was moving. Closing the distance between us, I placed my hand on his arm, trying to offer comfort. "I'm so sorry. I can't imagine how terrifying that must have been."

"I can't lie. It fucked with me for a while. The guy who took us was shot and killed in the midst of everything, and for a long time, I would have nightmares about those gunshots. Part of becoming a cop was me wanting to take that power back for myself."

"That's incredibly brave of you."

"Trick was the one who saved us. As soon as he found out we were missing, he put together a team and turned the whole damn town upside down to find us." He let out a chuckle that was full of so much pain and anger, it grated like nails on a chalkboard. "A man who was no relation to us was ready to burn the world to the ground for us while the man who had a hand in creating us tried to run as soon as he found out we'd been taken."

I sucked in a pained gasp. "Tristan."

"We were in that situation because of *him*, and that fucker just took off. Tried to get out of town before anyone caught on. Trick found him before he could skip town. *That's* why Trick is our father. That other guy stopped existing for me the moment his choices put my sister's and my lives at risk."

I moved on instinct, closing the very last bit of

distance between us and wrapping my arms around Tristan's waist. He froze for the length of two heartbeats before lifting his arms and closing them around me, tightening the hug. It was the first time we'd touched in such a way. While the intimacy of the embrace made my heart race and my skin feel tight, I ignored the instinct clawing at me to let go and run out of there before things could go any further, stomping that feeling down.

It didn't matter I was drawn to the man in a way that felt exciting and dangerous at the same time. What I felt for him became stronger every day, scaring the absolute shit out of me.

It didn't matter, because this was what he needed. After sharing such a painful story, he needed care and comfort, and offering him that was the very least I could do, given all he'd done for Levi and me.

"If I knew all it took to get a hug from you was to share a sob story, I would have told you a long time ago."

I pulled back and pursed my lips, shooting him a glare. "Don't be a smartass."

I whipped around and stomped away from the island. "Wait, wait!" he called after me, humor dripping from his words. "Don't go."

I stopped and turned back to face him, crossing my arms over my chest.

"I need to tell you about the time I was playin'

dodgeball and got hit in the stomach so hard I peed my pants. It was an incredibly tragic moment that still scars me to this day." He lifted his arms out to his sides. "Hug it out?"

I flipped him off and stormed out of the kitchen, but as the sound of his laughter followed after me, I couldn't keep the smile off my face.

Chapter Fifteen

Tristan

I walked into the bullpen at work, my hands laden down with to-go cups from Muffin Top. Harrison's eyes brightened the second they landed on me.

He shot to his feet, arms outstretched. "Ah, you are a prince among men."

His brows pulled together when I yanked my arm back before he could grab one of the cups. I tsked and shook my head. "That'll be six dollars and fifty cents."

"*What?*"

"I might be a prince among men, but I'm not made of money, asshole. You want your coffee, pay up."

"Cheap bastard, can't just do something nice for his buddy." He grumbled a string of colorful curses at me from under his breath as he pulled his wallet from his back pocket and began riffling through. "All I got is a ten."

I extended the coffee his way and waited for him to take it so I had a free hand to pluck the bill from his fingers. "Consider the rest delivery fee and tip."

"You aren't Postmates, asshole," he called as I moved to my desk and took a seat. "See if I get *you* a coffee next time."

Harrison never stopped for coffee on the way into work, but wouldn't hesitate to text me his order in the mornings on the off chance I planned on going. That was why I didn't feel bad about taking his money.

I ignored my pouting partner and booted up my computer, ready to get to work.

"What's gotten into you this morning?" Harrison asked, staring at me from across our desks like I'd grown a third eyeball in the center of my forehead.

"What do you mean?"

"I mean you're *whistling*. It's eight in the morning. No one should be that goddamn cheerful."

I chuckled and shook my head. Harrison and I had been partners long enough that I was used to him being a surly asshole in the mornings. The man didn't people very well until he had at least one cup of coffee in his system.

"Nothing's gotten into me. I'm in a good mood."

What I didn't tell him was that my good mood was because of the hug Merritt had given me the night before. It might seem ridiculous to people on the outside that something as simple as a hug was enough to brighten my entire week. But those people didn't know Merritt. They wouldn't understand how major it was that she would initiate that type of contact.

Given everything she suffered through, it was understandable she'd shied away from touch when it came to me or other men. I'd been slowly testing my limits so I wouldn't risk doing something that might trigger her. A brush of the hand here, a short, friendly touch there. But I kept the lines very, very clear, and did not cross them until she showed me she was comfortable. She'd loosened up a great deal around me, but I didn't miss the way she'd subtly move off course in the grocery store aisle if a man was coming from the other direction, shifting closer to the shelves to make more space in the middle.

She did the same thing on sidewalks. She didn't mind the closeness with Blythe, but when Rhodes had swung by the house the other day to drop off a ratty old dresser Merritt and my sister had picked up at an estate sale, I noticed she'd unwittingly backed up when he breeched that invisible line she kept around herself. He'd noticed as well, but instead of making a thing of it, he'd quietly respected her space and made sure to stay back as far as she needed.

That hug she'd given me the night before was proof I'd gotten through those shields she had up. She'd let me in, and that trust she had in me was continuing to grow. I'd meant it when I told her that was a gift, and I couldn't put into words what it meant to me.

"I swear, you two bicker worse than an old married couple."

I lifted my head from my computer and grinned. "Mornin' Captain," I greeted.

"Stop being so chipper," Harrison groused. "It's not natural, damn it."

Hayes rolled his eyes at my partner's surliness. "No coffee yet?" he asked me.

"He's just started his first cup. Give him a few more minutes."

"Have I ever told you how much I love it when you guys talk about me like I'm not here?" Harrison clipped sarcastically. "Makes me feel all warm and fuzzy."

Our boss cut his eyes my partner's way and pointed at the paper cup. "Finish that before you say somethin' that pisses me off."

Harrison's face pulled into a pout, but he did as ordered and took several gulps as Hayes turned back to me. "Got some news that should make your mood even better."

"Oh?" I asked when he didn't continue.

"Judge just signed off on that TRO for your girl this mornin'. How you want to handle this?"

I didn't bother holding back my smile. "I think I'll serve this one myself."

"Thought you might say that," Hayes grunted. "Just . . . make sure you don't do anything that'll get your ass suspended, would you? I can't afford to be down a detective."

"Don't worry, boss. I've got it under control."

And there was no way in hell I was going to miss the look on that asshole's face when I informed him he wasn't allowed anywhere within a hundred yards of Merritt.

Harrison studied me from the passenger seat as we pulled up to the building where Warren Bell worked. I looked at the clock and saw it was just before 9:00. I'd timed it perfectly so we'd be serving him in front of an audience. I wanted to make the situation as humiliating for him as possible.

"You sure you got this locked down?" Harrison asked, pulling my focus from the front of the building where a steady stream of people trickled in. "Guys like him are good at getting under a person's skin. You can't react to anything he might say."

"Don't worry, man. I'm good. Promise."

We got out of the car and walked toward the building. The receptionist looked up, the instant smile she probably greeted everyone with slowly slipping as she caught sight of our expressions and badges. "Uh, good morning. H-how can I help you?"

I grinned, hoping to put her at ease. After all, it wasn't like we were here for her. "Good morning. Detectives Fanning and O'Neil here to see Warren Bell. Could you please call him out here?"

"Sure this," she chirped nervously.

I moved back to Harrison, who was scanning the lobby. He let out a low whistle when I reached his side. "Swanky digs he's got here." He kept his voice low so no one else could hear. "What'd you say this asshole does again?"

"Something in consulting," I answered. "So you know what that means."

"Bullshitter," we both said at the same time. Most of the time, when someone said they were in "consulting" it was because they couldn't give a definitive answer for what they did. I'd done some digging into Warren, but I hadn't been able to find out exactly what he "consulted" on, but he brought home a pretty nice paycheck doing it.

A few minutes later, the interior office door opened and the man in question stepped through. He gave the receptionist a smile that rivaled those of most car sales-men. "Thanks so much, Stephanie." Then he turned to us. "Good morning, officers. How can I help you?"

"Detective," I said in response, a grin that matched his own tilting my lips. He meant it as a slight, using the wrong title, and he most likely didn't think we were smart enough to catch it. That was how dickheads like him operated. But my expression told him I knew what he'd done. "But we wouldn't expect you to understand the difference."

I got an immense sense of satisfaction at the way his jaw ticked. *That's right, you shithead, I can dish it out just as well as you can.*

"And we're here for this." I extended the letter-sized manilla envelope his way. As soon as his fingers closed around it, I added, "Warren Bell, you've been served."

His head jerked up. "Excuse me?"

"This is a restraining order stating you're not to come within one hundred yards of your estranged wife, Merritt Bell."

The receptionist let out a squeak, and from the way

she ducked her head and snatched her phone up, I was sure the office grapevine had officially gone into effect. No doubt news of this would be all over the building by lunch.

Warren's face began to turn a splotchy red as he fought to maintain his composure. "This has to be some sort of mistake. Gentlemen, I can assure you, this is completely unnecessary." He turned up the charm, but it didn't hide the fact the mask he kept in place was beginning to slip. The laugh he let out sounded more manic than humorous. "My wife has these . . . spells. You see, sometimes her mind gets a little muddled. I'm sure we can all work this out."

I pulled in a deep calming breath. I was not going to lose my cool and do something to give the prick the upper hand. "And I can't assure *you*, this absolutely is necessary. At least according to the judge who saw the pictures of the bruises that covered a large portion of Ms. Bell's upper torso."

You can bet your ass I said that loud enough for the Snoopy Stephanie back there to hear.

Warren began to bluster. "How *dare* you! You have no right coming into my place of work and spreading filthy lies. I'll have your badge for this. You mark my words!"

"Consider them marked." I started to turn, but

stopped myself. "Oh, and as for your *estranged* wife and these so-called spells? Well, she's been living with me for almost three weeks now, and if you ask me, she's sharp as a tack."

"You fucking son of a—"

He attempted to lunge in my direction, but Harrison stepped in and got between us, blocking his path and stopping him with a hand to the chest. "I wouldn't do that if I were you. Not unless you want us to cuff you here in front of the lovely Stephanie"—he shot the woman a wink that made her blush, the fucking flirt—"and take you in for assaulting a police officer. Your morning's started off pretty rough already. If I were you, I'd quit while I was ahead."

My partner gave the man a beat to see if he'd heed the warning, and when it was clear there was no longer a risk, we turned and headed out the door.

"Christ, man. You had to mash that button, didn't you?" he grunted once we were out of the building and heading toward our car.

I couldn't stop the shit-eating grin that stretched across my face. "You know I did. Especially after all that shit he'd said about her."

He blew out a sigh as I beeped the locks, rounding the car and pulling open his door. "Can't say I blamed you. That was seriously fucked up." He turned to me and arched a brow. "That make you feel good?"

I let out a laugh. "Hell yeah it did."

Harrison smirked. "Good enough to stop off at Muffin Top for a couple coffees on the way back?"

I threw the car into gear without answering but ended up stopping off anyway, because the answer was, *yes*, I did feel that good.

Chapter Sixteen

Tristan

I turned onto my street, anticipation swirling in my stomach the closer I got to the house. Since Levi and Merritt moved in, I couldn't wait to get home at the end of the day so I could see them.

Over the past month, the three of us—well, the three of us and Doc—had fallen into an easy rhythm that had honestly become the best part of my day. I'd been a bachelor for so long and enjoyed the privacy that came with that. I'd never really looked at my future and thought about a wife and kids, but things were changing. Rather than going to the bar, I preferred to go home and watch Pay-Per-View wrestling with Levi. Instead of casually dating or looking for a one-night stand, I enjoyed spending my evenings with Merritt, each of us enjoying a drink at the end of the day as we wound down. Getting to know the woman who'd been consuming my thoughts for months was better than the thought of hooking up with anyone else.

I wanted to be with them. I enjoyed their company more than anyone else's.

I guided the Suburban into my driveway and saw that everyone was outside. Merritt was pacing back and forth along the front porch, while Levi lay in the front yard as Doc jumped around, pouncing on him as the two played.

I climbed out, my gaze bouncing between a giggling Levi and an anxious Merritt.

"Tristan's home!" Levi shouted exuberantly, like he hadn't seen me in weeks. It was the same way he greeted me every evening, and I had to admit, it felt damn good to have someone so excited to see me.

I braced for collision. That was a lesson I'd learned a long time ago with my own nieces and nephew that definitely benefited me with Levi. He launched himself at me like one of those wrestlers, and I managed to catch him before he could bust his head open. "Hey, kiddo. You have a good day?"

"Yeah, it was awesome! Matt Bernard fell off the monkey bars durin' recess and busted his nose. There was blood *everywhere!*"

I swallowed down my chuckle at his excitement at

seeing blood. It was such a little boy thing. Hell, a lot of grown ass men would get a kick out of the gore too.

"Was Matt okay?"

"Yeah, the nurse said he was gonna be okay, but he still got to go home early. *Lucky*," he said on a sulk, even though I was sure poor Matt Bernard wasn't feeling particularly lucky. But kids didn't consider stuff like that. At Levi's age, I'd been convinced I was made of rubber and totally indestructible.

I caught movement from the corner of my eye as I put Levi back on his feet, glancing over to see that Merritt was still pacing, and she'd started chewing on her thumbnail.

"You and Doc keep playin', buddy, I'm gonna go have a talk with your aunt."

"Okay." He picked up a stick in the grass and gave it a heave across the front lawn. "Doc, fetch!"

I moved up the walkway and took the steps that led up to the porch. "Everything okay?"

She stooped and spun around to face me. "We can't live here anymore."

My stomach bottomed out. Dread washed through me, reaching down my throat and squeezing my lungs. "What? Why? Look, whatever happened, I'm sure we can work it out." They couldn't leave. The thought of not having Levi's laughter and excitement filling the house scared me. I couldn't imagine walking around and not having Merritt's scent lingering in the air. Her intoxicating fragrance was everywhere. In every room. A hint of citrus and a smoky sweetness. Like orange peels and burnt sugar.

"Just talk to me. Tell me what happened."

"There's a spider in the house," Levi called out from the grass, his words bringing me up short and leaving me momentarily speechless.

"I'm sorry. What?"

"Yeah, Aunt Merri's super scared of spiders. She saw it, screamed really loud, yanked us outside, and locked the door."

I slowly turned back to face Merritt, arching a single brow.

"It's not *just* a spider," Merritt clipped defensively, crossing her arms over her chest. "It was huge! And it was this weird, milky white color, and kind of translucent. Like a demonic spider straight out of hell or something. I saw a web in that sideboard Blythe and I found at the estate sale. It could have laid eggs." She sucked in a started gasp. "They could have *hatched*."

I swallowed down the laughter desperate to come out. "And locking the door would prevent them from . . . chasing after you?"

"I don't know. I freaked out, okay" she declared,

throwing her arms out at her sides. "I'm scared to death of spiders, happy now? They aren't natural. Nothing on this planet should have that many legs. And some of them are fuzzy! I mean, what the hell is that? That's not right! I saw the thing and reacted. I got everyone out safely and locked the door. The house belongs to the spider now. Way I see it, there are only two choices."

"And those would be?"

"We either move or burn the house to the ground." She lifted her chin and gave me an indignant look. "What's it gonna be?"

I lost it, a deep laugh rolled all the way up from my stomach and burst past my lips like a cannon blast. I couldn't remember the last time I found something as funny as I did Merritt's irrational fear of spiders, and I laughed harder than I had in a very long time.

"Great," she grumped, her expression drooping. "And now you're laughing at me. Thanks a lot."

I got a hold of myself, my laughter sputtering out and leaving me breathless. "Ah, I'm sorry, Dandelion."

She glared viciously. "No you're not. You're still smiling." She jabbed a finger at my mouth.

She was too damn cute sometimes. Like when she pouted over losing at Sorry!. Or when she got testy because someone ate the last blueberry muffin. Now this. Every single thing about her left me intrigued and wanting to know more, and on that thought I realized I didn't just have feelings for the woman. I was falling for her. Dropping faster than the speed of sound. Only problem was, after everything she'd been through, she wasn't ready. And for the first time in my life, I wanted something serious. Something real and permanent.

It was just my luck that I wanted it with a woman who was unavailable.

That realization made my chest ache.

"Come here," I said, making myself feel better by grabbing her hand and pulling her into me. I tucked her against my chest and wrapped my arms around her, holding her close. And damn if it didn't feel right. I pulled in a deep breath, filling my lungs with that candied orange scent. "I'm sorry, Dandelion. I wasn't trying to hurt your feelings."

"It was a really big spider," she defended weakly, her words muffled against my chest, causing me to smile.

"I'm sure it was. Would it help if I went inside and got it out for you?"

She pulled back and looked at me like I just lost my mind. "Get it out? No! You need to kill it, Tristan. Send that thing straight back to hell where it belongs."

It defied logic, but just then, her little bout of crazy made me desperate to kiss her.

Fuck me. I was so screwed.

MERRITT

TRISTAN HAD BEEN true to his word. He'd gone inside while the rest of us remained in the front yard, and hunted the spider down. Knowing I wouldn't have just taken his word for it, he'd showed me its dead, squished body so there was no doubt. Then he took it a step further by spraying the antique sideboard I'd been storing in the sunroom off the back of the house until I could get around to restoring it for Blythe, killing anything that might have still been living in there and wiping all the webs out with a rag.

He'd done that all on his own, without me having to ask, simply because he knew it would give me peace of mind. By now, I'd lost count of all the things he'd done to make life easier for Levi and me, to make it better. I hadn't had anyone take care of me the way Tristan did since my mom got sick years ago.

It was getting harder and harder to ignore the way he made me feel. The little flutter in my belly that started up when I knew he was on his way home. The way my chest tightened when he called me Dandelion. The tingle beneath my skin whenever he touched me. With every passing day, I wanted more of him any way I could get it. And I could no longer convince myself it was because he was my friend.

He was more than that. I wasn't sure when it happened exactly. It just happened. So naturally it was almost as if it was meant to. But I couldn't ignore the tiny voice of doubt in the back of my head that told me it was too soon, that Tristan could still end up hurting me.

I was really starting to hate that voice.

"What are you thinking about so hard over there?"

I was startled out of my thoughts by Tristan's voice. I blinked and found him watching me from where he'd been sitting on the loveseat across the living room from me.

I'd come downstairs after tucking Levi in and curled up on the couch with one of my books, hoping that focusing on a story would help keep my mind from running wild about Tristan. He'd come down a little while later with his laptop and sat across from me, typing away on something while I attempted to read.

Only problem was that I hadn't gotten more than two pages into the story before my mind wandered again, and the path it drifted to was Tristan.

I wasn't sure how long I'd been sitting there, staring

at the same page, before he noticed. "Huh? Oh. Nothing. I must have spaced out."

His brows pulled together, his expression filled with concern. "You sure? You're not still worried about the spider, are you? I swear to you, I got everything. This house is completely spider free."

I grinned. "No. I'm not worried about the spider. I'm good. I promise. Just getting a little tired, I guess. I should probably head up to—"

Before I could finish my sentence, a sharp, terrorized scream wrenched through the entire house, turning my blood to ice.

The book I'd been holding fell to the floor when I shot up from the couch and ran to the stairs. Tristan was already in front of me, taking the steps two at a time in his rush to get up to Levi as he continued to scream. The fear I heard coming from my little guy twisted my insides and clenched my lungs in a vise grip.

It felt like an eternity to get to him, but in reality, it was barely a handful of seconds.

Levi was sitting up straight in his bed, his skin deathly pale. His eyes were wide with fear, but his glazed look told me he wasn't awake, he was trapped in the middle of a nightmare.

Tristan hit his knees right beside the bed as I sat on the edge of the mattress and reached for my nephew.

"Levi, honey. Hey. Hey, you're okay, baby. You're okay. I'm right here."

"No! *No no no!* I don't wanna go back!"

"Baby, wake up. Everything's okay. You're here with me. You aren't going anywhere."

"Don't let him take me! Don't let him take me!" he screamed with such terror it shredded at my heart. I knew who he meant, and it shattered me that the person he was so scared of, the one who gave him nightmares, was his own father. The very person who was supposed to protect him.

Tears burned in my eyes, breaking free and falling down my cheeks as I tried to get through to him. "You don't have to go back, Levi. I swear. You're never going back."

I still couldn't reach him, and the longer he stayed trapped, the harder my tears fell. Finally, Tristan pushed closer. I wasn't sure how, but he was the picture of calm to my utter panic.

"Dandelion, let me try."

I turned my face to his, his form blurred around the edges thanks to my tears. "Please," I croaked. "Help him."

His hand came up and caressed my face. "I'm here, baby. I've got you both." I shifted over on the bed so he could sit beside Levi. He plucked my nephew up like he weighed nothing and pulled him into his lap. He held him close, wrapping Levi in his arms so he couldn't hurt himself flailing around like he was. "Come on, buddy. Wake up," he said, his tone gentle and firm at the same time. "We're here, buddy. We've got you. You're safe, so it's time to wake up." Tristan began rocking him side to side in soothing motions, and it didn't take long for Levi to finally start calming down.

He blinked the haziness from his eyes, but the tears still tracked down his pale cheeks. The nightmare finally lost its grip, and he realized where he was. As soon as he saw me, he launched himself in my direction, and I didn't hesitate to wrap him up in my arms as his locked around my neck. "Aunt Merri," he whimpered, his voice scratchy and raw.

"I'm right here, baby. We're here. Me and Tristan. You're all right. It was just a bad dream, okay?"

He sniffled and burrowed deeper into me as the tension started melting from his little body. He was only a handful of minutes away from an adrenaline crash, and I wanted to be here for him when it happened.

"You want me to lie down with you until you fall back asleep, little dude?"

"I wanna sleep with you," he said, his voice already growing sluggish.

"Okay. No problem. Let's head to my room—"

He shot straight, pulling back so his eyes could scan the room, "And Tristan," he said quickly, a tinge of panic in his voice. "I want Tristan too. Can I sleep with you both?"

My eyes went wide as I met Tristan's gaze over Levi's head. "Oh, honey. I don't think—"

Tristan spoke up. "If that's what you need to get back to sleep, kiddo, that's what you'll get."

"*Are you sure?*" I mouthed to him. As messy as my head was when it came to my feelings for Tristan, if this was what Levi needed to feel safe again, I'd make sure he got it. Nothing else mattered to me more than him.

Tristan nodded, then reached out and took Levi from me. He stood from the bed with my nephew wrapped around him like a koala. "We'll crash in my room tonight. I have the biggest bed. It'll be like a sleepover."

I made sure Levi was tucked soundly in the very middle of Tristan's large bed, and as I went through my nightly routine to prepare to go to sleep, I tried to look at it that way, like it was just a fun sleepover.

But my stupid heart refused to get on board.

Chapter Seventeen

Merritt

I felt like I was walking around in a daze as I moved from room to room at Second Hope Lodge. I cleaned the guest rooms on autopilot since there was one person occupying every inch of space in my brain. He had been for weeks now, and it had only gotten more intense since waking up this morning wrapped in his arms.

After Levi's nightmare the night before, I thought there wasn't a chance in hell I was going to get any sleep. But with Levi pressed against me and Tristan's soothing cloves and spice scent wrapped around me, I was out almost as soon as my head hit the pillow.

I couldn't remember the last time I slept so soundly, and as scared as I was to admit it to myself, I knew why— or *who*—made that possible. I knew it was because he made me feel safe, made it possible for me to let go of the fear and stress so I could rest easy for the first time in years.

I don't know how it happened, but at some point in the night, Levi and I managed to switch places, and I ended up in the middle of the bed. When I woke up, my back was pressed into Tristan's chest. His arm was like a steel band around my waist, and our legs were tangled together.

That was the first time I'd ever slept wrapped up so securely with someone else. Warren had claimed early on that he wasn't much of a cuddler. I'd been disappointed for a while, wanting to feel that kind of closeness with him. However, it became a relief later on, once I discovered who and what he really was. The last few years of our marriage, I'd slept every night curled up in a tight ball at the edge of the bed, as far away from Warren as I could get. I was always on guard, even in my sleep; the slightest movement from his side of the bed had me shooting awake.

I didn't need to do that with Tristan. It was like I knew instinctively I didn't have anything to fear, so my body relaxed in a way it hadn't in a very long time.

I'd spent most of my day so far replaying how I'd woken up. The way his arms tightened when I shifted, like unconsciously he didn't want to let me go, caused my belly to clench in a needy way I hadn't felt in far too long, and when he nuzzled into my hair and inhaled deeply, letting out a rumbly moan, I had to bite my lip to keep from whimpering.

When he murmured, "Mornin', Dandelion," in that raspy, sleep-rough voice, I nearly spontaneously combusted. I was so screwed, because I didn't know how the hell I was supposed to go back to sleeping in my own bed after the most perfect night's sleep of my life, and an even better wakeup call.

My body still reacted to the memory of it, even hours later. Every time I thought back to all those hard, warm muscles, that intoxicating scent, and that more-than-impressive morning erection that had been prodding me in the back, I became hot all over.

Like I was in that very moment.

Damn it.

I'd slipped into the daydream again, and when I blinked back into reality, I was clutching the clean sheets I'd been using to make the bed in a death grip. I needed to get my shit together. I was behaving like a hormonal teenager, not a grown woman who was supposed to have more self-control than this.

I shook off the Tristan-induced daze and got back to work. I made the bed with the sheets I'd been strangling, relieved I was able to stretch out the wrinkles that had formed from my fists, and moved on to dusting. I had just started on the bathroom when I heard voices coming from outside the room I was in.

"I didn't need you to tag along to keep an eye on me. You do realize I'm a grown-ass woman, right?"

"Who said anything about keeping an eye on you?" another woman asked. "Maybe I wanted to meet her too. Ever consider that?"

Meet who? I thought. The conversation happening in the hallway outside the room was more than a little intriguing.

"Please," the first voice scoffed, and I imagined the woman was rolling her eyes. "I don't buy it. You're here to play babysitter."

The second woman blew out a raspberry. "Len, you know I love your personal brand of sass, but you also know you can come on a little strong sometimes."

Woman Number One—*Len?*—made an affronted sound. "I do *not* come on a little strong. I'm just . . . unexpected."

"You're great. Honestly. And you know I love you. But the longer we stand out here arguing about this, the weirder the situation is going to seem."

My curiosity got the best of me then, and I moved through the room, popping my head through the open doorway. "Um . . . hi."

They both let out startled yelps and whipped around to face me.

"Oh my God," the one on the left said. She was the owner of the second voice, a stunning woman with high-lighted brown hair and lighter brown eyes. Her cheeks flushed with embarrassment as she said, "We're so sorry. We thought you were in that room over there." She pointed to the room beside the one I was currently working in. The housekeeping cart I was using was parked between the two rooms, and I'd propped both doors open for easy access, so it was an understandable mistake.

I assumed the two women were guests, and didn't want to make them feel uncomfortable. I smiled, hoping to ease some of the second woman's discomfort. "It's no problem. Is there something I can help you with? Maybe more towels for you room, or—"

"Oh!" Woman Number Two let out a laugh. "No. Nothing like that. We actually wanted to introduce ourselves."

My brows pulled together. "To who?"

The other woman had thick, glossy black hair, and the most striking deep, forest green eyes I'd ever seen. They popped even while they were narrowed on her friend. "So you are *terrible* at this," she declared before turning her attention to me and smiling so big you would have thought I was an old friend she hadn't seen forever. "I'm Lennix. And this walking bag of awkward is my sister-in-law, Rae. Our family owns and operates the lodge and ranch."

My eyes widened. "Oh! You're more Paulsons." So far I'd met Rory, Becky, and Cord. Though Becky wasn't technically a Paulson since she was Rory's mother. Her last name was Hightower. I learned that the ranch was originally in the Hightower family. Then Rory married Cord Paulson, and, years later, their son Zach, took over the ranch. Since then, they'd expanded, and built the resort that was Second Hope. But they were all one big happy family, and they were all incredibly sweet. At least the ones I'd already met.

"Sure are," the woman I now knew as Rae said proudly. "I'm married to Zach."

"And I'm the baby of the whole brood." Lennix gave me a once over, scanning me up and down in a way that made me feel like I was part of an exhibit before declaring out of nowhere, "You're really pretty."

My lips formed an O. "Um . . . thank you?"

"Oh, it was a compliment, for sure. You're like, seriously gorgeous. With the dark hair and light eyes, you've got this whole Snow White vibe happening right now."

I really wasn't sure how to respond to that. Fortunately, I didn't need to, because Lennix wasn't finished.

"Word around town is that you're shacking up with Tristan Fanning. I've known that guy basically my whole life, since our moms are besties. There's a lot of that around here, you'll see. Anyway, he's like a brother to me, so I totally don't see him that way. There's no need to get territorial or anything." I hadn't even realized my whole body had gone stiff at her mention of Tristan. And sure enough, something territorial was stirring in my gut that must have been written all over my face. "But even though I'd never go there in a million years, because, *ew*, I'm not blind or dead, so I'm well aware how hot he is."

Rae threw her arms up in exasperation. "See, this is exactly what I meant when I said you could come on a little strong. Ivy's going to kick your ass if you scare her off. And she's got that crazy pregnancy strength right now. She could totally do it."

Lennix waved her hand at her sister-in-law while I stood there, wondering if I should find the whole situation hilarious or odd. I was leaning toward the former.

"You shush," she ordered, then to me she said, "My curiosity has been driving me crazy. I have to know, what's he like in bed?"

I proceeded to choke on my own spit.

"You know what? Ignore me." Rae suddenly changed her tune, her curiosity piquing as well. "Lennix had the right idea. You see, he comes off as this great, super trustworthy guy. Like, he's the dude you'd call if a pipe busts in your kitchen or something, and he drops everything to come fix it for you. But then there's this swoon vibe beneath that, he's this big, strong, alpha protector who's capable of just . . ." She trailed off, and Lennix was all too happy to finish Rae's thought for her.

"Ripping your panties off with his teeth?"

"Yep! That."

My jaw hinged open, then closed, then opened again as I struggled to find the right words. All the while, I could feel heat creeping up my neck to my cheeks, and I knew I was probably glowing bright red.

"I . . . um . . ."

"You don't have to answer if you don't want," Lennix assured me. "I had to ask." She lifted her arms in a shrug. "Can't blame a girl for tryin' right?"

"No, it's just, well . . ." I bit down on my bottom lip. "We haven't . . . you know," God, I felt like I was in high school again. "We're just friends." Those words left behind a sour taste as I said them. It didn't come close to doing us justice. How I felt for Tristan was so much more complex than friendship.

They both seemed surprised by my admission. "Oh," Rae said after a few seconds.

Lennix crossed her arms over her chest. "Well, I gotta admit, I wasn't expecting that. I just figured . . .

you're hot. He's hot. You're under the same roof. Seemed like nature would take its course there."

My flush grew even deeper. My heart began beating a quick rhythm against my ribs.

Rae turned to Lennix. "And didn't Ray say Tristan got all possessive at the bar that night when she was brought up?"

Lennix snapped excitedly. "He did! Like he didn't want anyone else talking about her."

I held up my hands to stop them. "Wait. I thought you were Rae."

Rae smiled. "I'm Rae, R-A-E. We're talking about *Raylan*. He's the guy who handles the trail rides and fishing and other excursions around here."

That made sense. I'd met *that* Ray already. He seemed nice enough. Then something else they said hit me. "He didn't want other people talking about me?" I hadn't meant for my question to come out sounding as breathy as it had.

Rae and Lennix shared a look, matching knowing smirks curving their lips. "I believe Ray*lan*'s exact words were that he seemed really protective of you. And not just in a cop way."

Hearing that shouldn't have made my stomach feel like a million butterflies had just taken flight, but it did. That voice in the back of my head told me I shouldn't be happy, but this time, instead of listening to her, I slapped a piece of duct tape over her mouth and stuffed her into a closet.

I'd never been much of a poker player, and they clearly read everything I was feeling all over my face.

Lennix closed the distance between us and linked her arm through mine, leading me away from the room I'd been cleaning. "Oh, honey. We have *so* much to talk about. I think it's time for you to spill the tea. But over coffee, because I don't actually drink tea."

I twisted to look back at the guest room that was getting farther and farther away with each step. "I don't know. I really need to finish—"

"You're on lunch," she insisted. "And we aren't going far. The coffee shop off the lobby might not be as good as Muffin Top, but it's nothing to sneeze at."

"Ivy won't mind," Rae added. "In fact, I just texted her the bullet points, and she's on her way down. She wants to hear all about this too."

Lennix patted my hand before I could have second thoughts and smiled up at me. "I like you," she announced. "I can already tell. We're going to be good friends."

For some reason, I actually believed that.

And the thought didn't scare the hell out of me. I found myself actually looking forward to it.

Chapter Eighteen

Tristan

Everything about Rochelle Winslow's lobby felt like it belonged on the ground floor of a Manhattan high-rise, not tucked away in a single floor building in the middle of our small rural town.

I didn't know much about interior design, but from where I stood, it was obvious this Rochelle woman had some taste. The whole place screamed class and sophistication.

"Tristan," Merritt whispered my name. "I don't know about this." I turned from the decor to the woman standing beside me. Apprehension was pouring off of her in waves, uncertainty swam in those pale sage eyes.

"Hey." I reached out and took her chin between my fingers, gently turning her head to meet my gaze. "If you're not ready for this, that's fine. We're moving at a pace you're comfortable with here. Just say the word and we're out."

I'd accepted the fact that there wasn't anything I wouldn't do for this woman. Even if it meant cancelling our appointment with one of the top family lawyers in the area. As much as I hated the idea of her remaining married to that fucker for longer than absolutely necessary, I'd do whatever she felt most comfortable with.

"No, it's not that. I'm ready for this, believe me." My shoulders slumped with relief. "It's just . . ." Her gaze darted from mine as she admitted, "I don't think I'll be able to afford this woman."

My thumb traced along her jawline. "Dandelion, that isn't somethin' you need to worry about."

Her eyes flared, then narrowed. "Of course it's something to worry about. People tend to get upset when they don't get paid for a job they've done," she snapped at me.

I chuckled, happy to see a bit of that fire in her return. Even if it was directed at me. I'd let her burn me day after day if it kept that fire going and prevented her from closing in on herself again. I couldn't stand the thought of her reverting back to the shell of the Merritt when we first met.

"I mean, you don't have to worry about it because it's already being taken care of."

She stepped away from my touch and slammed her hands down on her hips. "Tristan Fanning. What did you do?" she asked in a tone that was scarily reminiscent of the one my mom used on me more times than I could count growing up.

"It wasn't only me," I defended. "It was Blythe too." I held up my hand before she could argue. "And before you say you can't accept, or that it's too much, or find any excuse not to let us help, you should know, it won't matter. The retainer's already been paid."

And it was a small fortune. But there wasn't any amount my sister and I weren't willing to shell out to get Merritt free of that monster. Rochelle Winslow was the best, and Merritt needed the best. I had no doubt Warren was going to try and make this as painful as possible, and my girl needed someone capable and willing to go to the mat and fight for her so she didn't have to do it herself.

She scowled, doing her best to remain mad, but I could see she was wavering. "I can't believe you'd do that. I could never ask—"

I took one long stride, closing the distance she'd put between us and cupped her cheeks in my hands, bringing my face close to hers. "That's the point, sweetheart. You never would have asked. You would have worked yourself to the bone and sacrificed to try and do it yourself. But you don't have to do that. You aren't alone anymore, Merritt. You have people who want to help, who care about you." My throat worked on a swallow. "*I* care about you," I stressed, my voice gruffer than normal. "I don't regret what I did. I'd do it again a million times over. And so would Blythe."

The way she melted into my touch made it so hard not to lean in and kiss her the way I'd been dreaming of for weeks. It sparked to life the part of me I'd struggled to keep snuffed out, that part that wanted her more than I wanted my next breath. Keeping that in check had been a battle since the moment I met her, but it had gotten so much worse since the morning I woke up with her in my arms. That one night with her in my bed was all it had taken for me to become addicted, and I hadn't slept for shit without her in the two weeks since.

That candied orange peel scent that lingered on my sheets and pillow had helped, but once the smell of her faded away, I spent my nights tossing and turning. I had it so damn bad I'd considered sneaking into her room to find her perfume, so I could spray it all over my bed.

"You just keep getting better," she said on a quiet breath.

"What?"

"Every time I think you couldn't possibly get any better, you do something like this to prove me wrong. I keep waiting for the other shoe to drop. Keep searching for something hidden beneath the surface. But there isn't anything hiding, is there?"

It broke my heart that she'd suffered so much she now struggled to trust the good in people . . . in *me*. But I couldn't deny that it felt damn good to know she was starting to trust her gut when it came to me.

"No, Dandelion. There's nothing there. This is just who I am. But you take as much time as you need to believe it. I'm not going anywhere."

Her hands came up and her delicate fingers wrapped around my wrists. "I think I already believe it."

Christ, she was killing me. I started to lean in, her lips calling to me like a siren, when a throat cleared from behind us and broke the spell.

A string of curses colorful enough to make a sailor blush flew through my head on fast forward as I gritted my teeth and lowered my hands from Merritt's face.

We turned together to face the woman standing a few feet away, and just like the lobby, Rochelle Winslow dripped with class. The bold red of her skirt suit complemented the dark brown of her skin, but it also managed to make a serious statement, and what it said was *power*. Her heels cost more than one month's paycheck. Tight dark brown curls framed her face and jawline. Her makeup was flawlessly applied, and her expression gave absolutely nothing away as she studied the two of us like a specimen beneath a microscope. One perfectly arched brow rose as she asked, "Ms. Bell, I presume?"

Merritt cleared her throat and stepped away from me like we'd got caught making out in the school library. She wiped her palms on the thighs of her slacks as her cheeks pinkened under the woman's scrutiny.

Fuck, even I had to admit, she had me more than a little intimidated, but I managed to keep from squirming and held my stance.

"Yeah. Yes. Sorry. I'm Ms. Bell. I mean Merritt Bell. But please, call me Merritt. Everyone does. Because it's my name." She let out a manic laugh that only made her discomfort that much more noticeable.

I couldn't watch her flounder and not do something to help. Reaching out, I took her hand in mine and brushed my thumb over the rapid pulse in her wrist. "Hi. This is Merritt, and I'm Tristan Fanning. I'm the one who called to make the appointment."

Ms. Winslow watched me for one heartbeat. Then two. I got the impression she was taking my measure.

"Of course. It's good to meet you both. If you'll follow me, my assistant has prepared the conference room. We'll get right to it."

She turned on her heel without another word, expecting we'd follow. Merritt met my gaze and bugged her eyes out, mouthing, *"Wow,"* in a dramatic way that made me smile as we followed Merritt's new attorney, hand-in-hand.

Apparently, preparing a conference room consisted of ordering a large assortment of pastries and coffee, along with water, juice, and soda. The table seated at least twelve, however the rest of it was untouched, except for the seats closest to the door. There was a folder in front of the rolling chair at the head of the table and another by the first chairs on either side.

She waved a hand at the table. "Please, take a seat. And feel free to help yourself to something to eat and drink."

I knew Merritt well enough to know she'd be too anxious to eat, so I reached across the spread to pluck up a bottle of her favored grape juice and passed it to her. Her eyes flared with surprise in that way they always did when I did something or took notice of something in a way she hadn't expected.

A small part of me liked being able to surprise her like that, because it meant I'd made her happy. But a bigger part bristled every time I saw it, because that selfish son of a bitch had neglected her to the point that she was more used to fading into the wallpaper than being noticed.

I helped myself to a cheese danish and a cup of

coffee before plucking up the folder on the table across from Merritt and moving around to take the chair beside hers.

Ms. Winslow watched the whole thing, not that I could tell what the hell she was thinking with that blank look on her face.

"Before we go any further, I need to know exactly what's going on between the two of you." She looked our way, pointing her finger between Merritt and me.

I felt Merritt stiffen, her back shooting straight. "W-what do you mean?"

"I mean, are you together? And if so, who all knows? Did this start before or after you left your husband"—she flipped open the folder in front of her and took a quick glance—"roughly three and a half months ago and moved to Maryland?"

From the corner of my eye, I could see Merritt's cheeks go from pink to pale. "No. We aren't together. We're friends."

Ms. Winslow lifted that brow again. "But you are living together."

"Y-yes, but—"

I cut in, the discomfort the woman was causing setting my blood to a simmer. "Merritt initially left Hope Valley to escape a husband who had been abusing her for years," I clipped, anger clear in my tone. Merritt noticed too, because she reached under the table and placed her hand on my knee to offer comfort. "She moved in with me when she was ultimately forced to return in order to care for her nephew after her brother overdosed and eventually ended up behind bars. She had no other place to stay, and given that she was important to my sister, I offered up my home for two reasons. The first was that I simply wanted to help. The second was that I wanted to keep her safe." That was at least partially true. But I didn't think this woman needed to know I'd been just a bit obsessed with Merritt from the start.

Ms. Winslow sat back in her chair, doing that thing again where she took silent stock before coming to a decision or a judgment. It was disconcerting, to say the least, but I imagined it worked like a charm in court.

"Mr. Fanning, I assure that I mean no disrespect in my line of questioning. I don't care one way or another if you two are involved. Personally, given the animal your husband appears to be, Ms. Bell, I'm kind of hoping there is. I only need to know everything if I'm going to represent you to the very best of my abilities. That means no secrets that could pop up and blindside me. I must warn you, I'm not a fan of being blindsided. It tends to make me cranky."

I had a feeling this woman was not someone you wanted to fuck with when she was cranky.

"Would it be a problem if there was something happening between us?" I asked, the words spilling free before I could stop them.

Merritt's gaze whipped to mine, her eyes wide with surprise at my question.

I cleared my throat and tugged at my collar. "I mean, for the sake of argument." I hadn't meant to say the words out loud, but now that they were out there, I was desperate for the answer.

Chapter Nineteen

Merritt

With the way my heart was racing, I was surprised it hadn't jumped right out of my chest to dance a jig on the table right in front of us.

"Any other couple, I might say yes," Rochelle answered, pulling me out of a tailspin before I could get sucked down too far. I turned back to the woman who'd been intimidating the hell out of me since the moment we met. There wasn't a single doubt in my mind that Rochelle Winslow wasn't a shark in the courtroom. "As long as nothing started before you left the state—"

"It didn't," I interrupted. "I didn't even know him before I left."

She tapped her pen about the table. "Well then, given the fact that you currently have a restraining order against him for domestic abuse, which was filed along with actual photographic evidence, his attorney could try to make a big deal out of this, but I don't think it would sway a judge."

Why did that response make my heart flip? It almost felt like we were being given permission or something.

I gave my head a shake to clear it of those thoughts. This wasn't the time or the place for something like that.

"Merritt, I know this might be hard, but if it's possible, I'd like to hear about your relationship with your husband."

"Estranged," Tristan said on a growl. My fingers on his knee clenched, hoping to ease the strain in his features.

"Estranged husband," she amended with another cock of that one brow. I don't know how she did it, arching one brow at a time, and without a single wrinkle creasing her forehead. She shifted her focus back to me. "If you could tell me what it was like, as much or as little as you're comfortable sharing. I need to get a sense for how bad things were and the kind of man your estranged husband is."

That familiar anxiety began creeping in. I brought both my hands onto the table and clenched them into fists until my nails dug into my palms. Before I could break the skin or make sores, Tristan was there, using his thumb to ease my fingers apart and rub soothing circles against my skin. I didn't realize what I was doing until he stopped me, and that this wasn't the first time he'd done it.

He paid attention and was there to stop me from hurting myself, even if I was unaware I was doing it.

I curled my fingers around that thumb and held on like it was my lifeline as I answered, "I'll tell you as much as I can. The problem is, if you ask anyone else, my husb"—I caught myself and back-pedaled—"Warren is this perfect, nice, caring man to many. He has a gift for charming anyone into thinking he has a heart of gold."

Only I knew the truth. At least until a handful of people started trickling into my life who believed me.

Something flashed across her face, but she schooled her features before I could recognize what it was. "Rest assured, that's not something you have to worry about. I'm familiar with Warren Bell." It almost looked like she sneered as she said his name. "I'm familiar with that whole good old boys club he's a part of, and I'm aware of how those men function."

"I take it you're not a fan," Tristan pointed out.

"Of that group of spoiled, rich, white, trust fund bros who expect the world to be handed to them on a silver platter? Um, no. I am most definitely not a fan. I attended college and law school with a number of them.

It was hard to keep their true natures in check when they kept getting bested by a woman. An educated black woman, to be precise. I checked every box of the things they hated, and they couldn't stand it that I made better grades or that the professors liked me more. They got off on saying it was because I spread my legs, when the truth was, I wasn't a lazy, self-important pain in the ass."

She couldn't have described Warren and his friends any better if they'd been standing right in front of her holding signs listing all their worst traits.

My brows dipped into a worried frown. "Are you sure you want to do this? To deal with Warren after all of that? I wouldn't blame you if you didn't want to go down that road again."

"Are you kidding?" For the first time since meeting her, she showed a hint of emotion. Her lips stretched into a smile so predatory it sent a shiver down my spine. "I'll take any chance I can get to knock those preppy golden buddies down a few pegs. I'm all in. By the time I finish with him, that man will be lucky if he's left with the clothes on his back."

"I don't need all that. I just want to be done with him. I want a divorce."

"Oh, sweetie, you'll get it. Believe me. But I'm also going to make it hurt."

The meeting lasted another hour and a half, and by

the time it was over, I was drained. Having to relive those six miserable years syphoned off every bit of energy I had, leaving me feeling numb. With every story I told, the energy radiating off of Tristan grew heavier and heavier until the air in the room felt suffocating. If I thought for a second that I could get away with it, I'd crawl into my bed as soon as we got back to the house and pull the covers over my head for the next two days. But I already knew Tristan wouldn't allow that.

As it was, I felt his eyes drilling into the side of my face every few minutes as we drove away from my new lawyer's office.

"You've been quiet since we left the office," Tristan said a while later, breaking the silence that had filled the Suburban the entire drive so far. "If you don't want to talk, feel free to tell me to mind my own business, but I need to know you're all right."

The sigh I let loose felt like it drained my lungs of oxygen. "I'm tired. And I'm mad," I admitted, getting to the root of everything that had been swirling around inside me for the past couple hours. The more I thought about it, the madder I got, and as strange as it might have been, I actually preferred the anger over the numbness. I'd spent all those years with Warren numbing myself in order to survive. I'd take feeling anything over that.

"No, you know what? I'm not just mad. I'm pissed!"

Tristan cast me a curious look before looking back to the road. "You want to talk about it?"

"Going through everything with Rochelle just reminded me of how long I spent trapped with that monster. I'll never get those years back. I met him when I was barely twenty-one. My most formative years are just gone!"

His brows pinched together. "Well, I wouldn't say they were all your formative years. You're still young, Dandelion. There's a whole lot of life left to live."

"I get that, but it's not only that those years are gone. I'm also mad I spent them being scared and lonely and sad. The more I told Rochelle, the more I realized those were the only emotions I felt, Tristan. For six years, there was nothing but fear, loneliness, and sadness."

"Baby," he rasped out, that one word coming out thick with pain. His jaw ticked as his fingers clenched the steering wheel. Despite the agony in his voice and etched onto his face, I couldn't help but feel a flutter of pleasure at him calling me baby. It wasn't quite as good as Dandelion, but there was an intimacy to it that warmed me from the inside out.

His hand shot across the center console and grasped mine, lacing our fingers together and bringing them across so he could rest them both on his thick, strong thigh. "I could kill him for making you feel that way," he said in a low growl as he visibly fought to keep himself in check. I'd seen him do that more than once, and I knew he was trying to rein in his anger so he didn't do or say something to scare me.

But he couldn't scare me. Not anymore. If there was one person on this planet I trusted above everyone else, it was Tristan Fanning. He was the best man I'd ever known, and I knew down to my very soul he would never hurt me. He'd proven that time and time again.

"When I think about what he did to you—"

I twisted in my seat and pulled my hand free of his so I could wrap it around the back of his neck. It would have been so much easier to comfort him if we weren't driving, but I'd make do. "Don't think about it."

"Merritt—"

"I'm serious, Tris. Stop thinking about it. I've decided that's what I'm going to do."

He cast a skeptical look in my direction. "Just like that, huh? You make it sound easy."

I pressed my fingers into his skin before dragging them up into the hair at the nape of his neck. It was the first time I touched his hair. I'd wondered for weeks what his hair felt like, and now I knew it was just as soft and silky as it looked. He leaned into my touch like it provided him with comfort.

"I didn't say it was going to be easy. It'll probably be

hard as hell. But I'm going to do it anyway. You know why?"

I felt the tension in his neck start to melt away, and when he glanced my way, there was a tiny smile playing on his lips. "Why's that, Dandelion."

I returned his smile. As soon as I made that decision, it was as though a weight lifted off my chest. It was the strangest sensation, both scary and thrilling at the same time.

"Because I'm strong enough now to take my life back."

"Baby . . ." I was really starting to like that word. "You've always been strong. Strongest woman I know."

My insides began to melt. "Okay then, because I finally believe I'm strong enough to take my life back. How's that?"

He answered by pulling my hand from the back of his neck and bringing it around to press a kiss to my knuckles. Then he intertwined our fingers again. I was getting the sense that Tristan was big on hand holding, and I did not dislike it. "That's great, Merritt. I'm so fucking proud of you."

I made another decision in that very moment.

As soon as he pulled to a stop at a red light, I leaned a little closer to him and lowered my voice. "Ask me why I believe I'm strong enough, Tristan."

His head whipped in my direction, that pale blue in his eyes darkening as a million different emotions swirled inside their depths. "Merritt . . ."

"Ask me. Please."

His throat worked on a swallow and his nostrils flared on a deep inhale before he finally spoke softly, asking, "Why do you believe you're strong enough?"

"Because of you."

His hand shot out, wrapping around the back of my neck and pulling me toward him so he could rest his forehead against mine. He squeezed his eyes closed, his features a twisted mixture of pain and pleasure.

I don't know how long we sat like that before he finally opened his eyes again and stared straight into mine.

"That's the best gift anyone has ever given me, Dandelion. And I'll cherish it as long as I live."

Chapter Twenty

Merritt

My heart was racing a million miles a second. I wiped my clammy palms on the legs of my jeans as I stared at the ominous building through my windshield, but it didn't do any good. As soon as I was done, they were sweaty all over again.

My phone vibrated in the cup holder with an incoming text, jolting me out of my haze.

Tristan: You make it there okay?

I smiled, the stress that had been resting heavy on my shoulders all morning lessening as my thumbs moved over the screen, forming a reply.

Me: Made it safely. Just sitting in my car, trying to find the nerve to go in.

Those little dots at the bottom of the screen started

bouncing immediately. I pulled my bottom lip between my teeth as I waited for his response to pop up. Something had changed between us since that moment in Tristan's car two days ago. It felt like our relationship had gone from platonic to something . . . more. He didn't shy away from touching me, but it was different now. Now it was like there was a magnetic pull between us, drawing us closer whenever we were in the same room. He couldn't seem to stay away from me, not that it bothered me in the slightest. Truth was, I couldn't bring myself to stay away from him either. I didn't want to.

I kept thinking back to when he'd grabbed my neck and pulled me close. For a moment, I thought he was going to kiss me, and instead of being scared to death, I'd wanted it. I'd been dying for him to kiss me for a while, so when he pressed his forehead against mine instead, I was disappointed. And as each day passed since he didn't kiss me, that disappointment grew.

The buzz of my phone brought me out of the memory.

Tristan: Remember what a dandelion symbolizes. You're the strongest person I know, and I'm in awe of you every single day.

I don't think he would ever understand how much his faith in me meant. When I told him what I planned to do, he'd asked if I wanted him to come with me. I appreciated the offer, but as much as I didn't want to do this, I also knew it was something I needed to do by myself.

I glanced up at the building, at the chain link fences that wound around everything like a complicated maze, at the ominous razor wire looped along the top from end to end.

Despite the shining sun and the beautiful blue sky, the dull gray building and all that metal made everything seem dreary. This was the last place I wanted to be. But I had to do this. Not for myself, but for Levi. And the sooner I got it over with, the sooner I could get the hell out of there and back to my life. A life that was only getting better with every passing day. A life full of happiness.

The rules for getting into a prison were much more detailed than I would have thought, considering the guards spent their time trying to keep the prisoners in. I had to stand in a line with family members and loved ones of the other convicts. Visiting hours were limited, and because my brother had never been one to follow the rules, he'd been getting in his fair share of trouble, which resulted in him being thrown into solitary confinement regularly, so getting in to see him had been difficult.

This was the very last place I wanted to be, but I told

myself I'd give him this one last consideration, one last chance, then I was done.

After having my personal belongings taken from me until I left and being searched, I made it into a big, open room with metal tables and stools that were bolted to the concrete floor and bars on all the windows. There was a guard posted at the door the visitors came through, and another at the door where the prisoners entered. A third guard wound through the tables, watching everything that was happening.

The metal seat was freezing when I sat, sending a chill up my spine. I pulled in a fortifying breath and clasped my hands together in my lap as I waited for Ozzy to come through the door. I started to worry maybe he wasn't coming, when he finally stepped through. I sucked in a sharp gasp at my first look at him. He'd already been skinny, thanks to the heroine, but it was even worse now. He walked with a limp, and was sporting a swollen black eye that looked like it hurt like hell.

His hair hung limp over his forehead, and as I searched, I couldn't find a single similarity between him and Levi. Despite the guilt, I couldn't help but be thankful for that.

His good eye widened as soon as he saw me before narrowing into a glare. He moved to my table and plopped down on the stool across from me like it was an inconvenience to have to come and talk to me. I couldn't possibly imagine what he had to do with his day that was more important.

"Took you long enough to come for a visit."

My mouth opened and closed, then opened again. "I'm sorry. Have you been expecting me?" It wasn't like he'd ever had any use for me before. My brother never had time for me unless he wanted to pawn his son off or hit me up for money.

"It's not a stretch that you'd want to take the time to make sure your brother's okay after he gets locked up. But I guess you're too busy out there livin' that fancy life of yours to give a shit about me," he sneered.

My jaw dropped in shock. "My fancy life? Are you kidding me? Ozzy, the last time I saw you was when I came to say goodbye because I had to run from my abusive husband."

His lips pursed. "Well it doesn't look like you stayed gone for long. Guess you finally realized havin' the money for all those nice clothes and the cushy house and shit was worth takin' a couple hits."

The pain and betrayal I felt at those callous words slammed into me so hard I thought I might actually fall off the stool. "I-I can't believe you said that to me," I whispered, a knot forming in my throat as my eyes began to burn.

His lifted a shoulder in an insolent shrug. "Hey, don't blame me for thinkin' it. You're the one who came back."

Something inside me snapped, and I jerked forward, banging my palm against the metal table loudly. "I came back to take care of your son! A son you haven't bothered asking about, by the way."

He waved me off and sat back, crossing his arms over his chest. "I'm sure I'd have heard somethin' if there was a problem."

I couldn't believe the gall of the man sitting across from me. I knew my brother had an addiction, and I always thought that was the reason behind his cold nature and lack of empathy. I told myself over and over that, underneath the poison twisting his mind, he really loved me. But now I saw it for what it was. He didn't care. Not about anyone but himself. The boy who'd spun us around on the merry-go-round over and over again until we both fell off laughing then proceeded to puke our guts up, was gone. I didn't see a hint of him in there anywhere.

"You really don't care about him at all, do you? He's your son, Ozzy." I didn't bother hiding the disgust in my voice.

"Listen, I didn't want the kid in the first damn place, okay? But Cindy wouldn't get rid of it. Then her ass bailed, and I was stuck with him."

I didn't understand. Levi was the perfect kid. He was so full of love and light and happiness. I couldn't wrap my head around the fact that there would be anyone out there who didn't fall in love with him as soon as they got to know him, let alone his own father. There wasn't anything I wouldn't do for that little boy. I would crawl across broken glass and bleed myself dry for him. A part of me hated my brother for what he'd become, he couldn't give that to his own flesh and blood.

My mom had refused to give up on him, even when she was so sick from chemo she couldn't get out of bed. She passed away believing the old Ozzy would come back, so after she died, I'd picked up that torch of hope and carried it all this time. But I was done. I couldn't fight and plead for someone to change at the expense of my own happiness anymore. I'd spent too long putting Warren and my brother first. It was time for that to change. I needed to prioritize myself if I wanted to make a good example for Levi.

"Look, I didn't come here to fight with you."

"Then why'd you come, huh? You want to make me feel like shit for not bein' as perfect as you?" He curled his top lip away from his teeth in contempt, and mocked, "Perfect little Merritt, always does everything right."

I couldn't let his words get to me. This wasn't about me. This was for Levi. And I was strong enough to do this, damn it.

"I came to ask you to sign over custody of Levi."

Ozzy's brows slammed together. "To who?"

"To me." My heart began to beat faster now that the words were out. "You said you never wanted him, and I do, Oz. I want to take care of him, to raise him. Please, sign over custody."

"What's in it for me?"

Just when I thought he couldn't get any worse, he found a way to top it. I blanked my face, taking a page out of Rochelle's book and masking everything I was feeling. "There's nothing in it for you, Ozzy. This is your chance to put someone before yourself. To finally do what's right for Levi."

He snorted, a calculating grin turning his lips up. "I don't know, baby sis. Looks like I've got somethin' you want. If he's really as important to you as you say, you'd be willin' to do anything."

I was willing to do anything. But what Ozzy didn't know was I already came in here expecting this to be a long shot. I was prepared to fight him for Levi, and this was one fight I wouldn't lose.

"I came here as a courtesy, because you're my brother. I wanted to give you a chance to do the right thing on your own. But make no mistake, Ozzy, I will get custody of Levi, and I will make certain that you never darken his doorway ever again. I will protect him from everything that could hurt him, including you, and when he's grown and starting his own family, you'll be nothing but a hazy memory."

He shot forward, but I didn't flinch. I refused to give him the satisfaction. "You self-righteous little bitch," he hissed viciously. "You think you can come in here and start makin' demands? It's because of you I'm in here in the first fuckin' place. You owe me, you stupid cunt!"

I couldn't fathom how he could possibly blame me for the fact that he overdosed and got himself locked up for endangering his child, but the twisted inner workings of my brother's brain were no longer my problem.

And I was done taking his abuse.

I stood up, turned my back on him, and started for the door.

"Don't you walk away from me, you fuckin' bitch!" Ozzy bellowed.

I heard a scuffle, but I refused to turn around. I was done. My brother no longer existed for me, and I wouldn't give him another second of my time.

Chapter Twenty-One

Tristan

I paced from the kitchen to the living room and back again for what felt like a million times as I waited for Merritt to get home. I lost count of how many times I looked at the clock on the wall, but it felt like the goddamn arms never moved.

I felt like I was coming out of my skin, and I didn't even have Levi there to take my mind off things since it was a school day. I tried to fill my time by cleaning out the garage so I could create a sort of make-shift workshop for her to restore antique furniture. She'd shared with me how it was something she'd learned from her mother, and missed working with her hands like that. I wanted to give it back to her. But I was so damn antsy I blew through the project and finished a lot sooner than I expected.

The more time that passed, the worse the scenarios running through my head became. There was nothing rational about how I felt. All I could think was how that asshole could say or do something to hurt her, and I wouldn't be there to protect her. I wished she would have let me go with her, but at the same time, I respected her need to confront her brother on her own.

I was seconds away from saying fuck it and driving to the prison any damn way, when I heard her car pull into the driveway.

I practically threw myself on the couch, snatching up a book that had been sitting on the coffee table without bothering to look at the cover and flipping it open so it didn't look like I'd spent the last few hours wearing a hole in the carpet.

I felt a judgmental tingle on the side of my face and glanced over to find Doc staring at me from his dog bed. "Don't give me that look. You have no right to judge. You can be just as pathetic." I lifted my brows. "Remember how you threw yourself on the ground and screamed when that cat took a swipe at you? Didn't come close to touching you, and you still freaked out."

Doc lowered his head back onto the bed.

"Yeah. That's what I thought."

The door opened a second later, and I lifted my gaze from the book I was pretending to read. "Hey." Now that she was standing right in front of me and I could see for myself that she was okay, I was able to pull in my first full breath since she left the house earlier this morning.

Merritt glanced down at the book then up to me. "Hi. What are you doing?"

"Nothing," I stated casually. "Just reading."

The corners of her mouth trembled. "You read romance?" Of course it was one of her books I snatched up. "Yeah, sure. I read a bit of everything. I have diverse tastes."

She curled her lips between her teeth to hide her smile. "The book is upside down."

Son of a bitch.

I slapped the cover shut and tossed the book back on the coffee table, giving up pretenses. I raked my fingers through my hair as I stood up from the couch. "I've been going out of my mind."

She moved toward me, her expression softening as she closed the distance. "Were you worried about me?"

I couldn't resist reaching out to touch her as soon as she was close enough. I tucked a strand of that dark, glossy hair behind her ear and trailed my fingers down her jaw before forcing myself to drop my arm to my side. "I always worry about you when I know you're going into a situation where you could end up hurt."

"There were guards everywhere. There was no way

he could have gotten to me," she attempted to reassure me.

"I don't just mean physically, Dandelion. Too many people have been indifferent to your feelings in your lifetime. I want to protect you in every possible way. I know I can't, like I know you're capable of taking care of yourself, I just can't stand the thought of anyone hurting you."

Something moved across her beautiful face just then. "Can I ask you a question?"

"You can ask me anything."

"That day in your car, when you pressed your forehead to mine. Did you want to kiss me?"

My heart shot up into my throat, making it hard to breathe all of a sudden. Her question lit a fuse inside me, setting my blood to an automatic boil. "What?"

"Did you want to kiss me?"

Her eyes pleaded with me to tell the truth, and there was nothing I could deny her. "More than I wanted my next breath."

Her chest rose on a soft gasp, and her sage green gaze went glassy. "What if I gave you a chance to do it over?"

A deep rumble moved up my throat as my hands came up to cradle her face. "Baby, I need you to be completely sure of what you're askin' me. There can't be any doubt or miscommunication."

"I don't have any doubts. Tristan, I want you to kiss me."

That was all I needed to hear.

Bringing my mouth down on hers, I brushed my lips over hers, once, twice, testing her limits to make sure it wasn't too much. When she didn't pull away, I increased the pressure, flicking my tongue out for that first small taste.

"Tristan?" Merritt breathed against my mouth, forcing my eyes open.

"Yeah, baby?"

"I'm not delicate. Please stop treating me like glass and kiss me."

The iron grip I maintained on my self-control these past few months snapped, and I slammed my mouth onto hers. My tongue swiped in and slid against hers, eliciting a moan from deep within her chest. The sound went straight to my dick, making me want more.

My hands slid farther back, tangling with the hair at her nape as I took her mouth harder, deepening the kiss. Her arms came up and wrapped around my neck and held on as I lost myself in the kiss, in her. I couldn't get enough. I never wanted it to end, and would have gladly suffocated if it meant I didn't have to stop.

Merritt pulled back and sucked in a deep breath as she whispered my name. "Tristan."

"I'm right here," I returned as I dragged my lips down the delicate column of her throat.

"I want you."

I jerked back at her declaration, my gaze colliding with lust-drunk sea green. My cock jerked, the tip already weeping with my need to be inside her.

I dragged my thumb across her jaw and over her swollen bottom lip. "No miscommunication, Dandelion. Remember?"

There wasn't anything I wouldn't give her, but I needed her words. "Take me to bed. Please. I need you to make love to me."

She let out a yelp and giggled when I reached down and grabbed her ass, lifting her feet off the ground and forcing her to wrap her legs around my waist.

She fit me perfectly, like she was only for me, and there wasn't a better feeling on the face of the earth than Merritt wrapped around me. She fisted my hair and peppered frantic kisses along my jaw and neck, anywhere she could reach, while I took the stairs as fast as I could to my bedroom.

As soon as her feet touched down on the floor at the foot of the bed, we went at each other, tearing our clothes and throwing them across the room until I was wearing nothing but my boxer briefs, the material barely containing my erection. Merritt stood before me in a lacy, navy-colored bra and matching lace panties.

"Beautiful," I breathed as I took her in, my eyes feasting on every inch of her. "You're a goddamn vision, Dandelion."

"Tristan, hurry," she pleaded in a needy voice that drove me wild. She reached for my cock, but before her fingers could wrap around it, I grabbed her by the wrist. Her gaze shot up to mine, her brows furrowing in confusion.

"We'll get to that, but there's something I need to do first."

"What?" Her question ended on a squeal when I picked her up and tossed her onto the mattress. With a wicked smile, I grabbed the delicate waistband of her panties and yanked them down her legs. "I need to taste you."

I dropped to my knees at the foot of the bed and pushed her thighs wide, taking in the glistening, swollen flesh of her perfect pussy.

"Tristan—oh my God!" she cried out when I sealed my mouth over her core and licked. My balls drew up the instant her sweet, honeyed taste coated my tongue, and I had to reach into my underwear and squeeze the base of my dick to keep from coming.

"Tristan, yes," she panted, her hips jerking up off the

bed as I alternated between sucking on her clit and fucking my tongue deep inside her. "So good. I-I, oh God, I'm going to come."

I needed her to fall over that edge, and I needed her to do it fast or I was going to lose it. Sucking her clit between my lips, I flicked it with the tip of my tongue, over and over as she shattered. As soon as that first one left her, I crawled up the bed and hovered over her, my face so close I took in each gust of air she blew past her lips and gave it back, sharing one breath. I pushed her legs farther apart with my knees and lowered my hips into the cradle of her thighs. The heat from her pussy against my cock nearly had my eyes rolling into the back of my head.

"Merritt."

At the sound of her name, her eyelids peeled open to half mast, then flared when my tip bumped against her entrance. "You sure you want this?"

Her hands came up and her fingers tangled in my hair. "I've never wanted anything more."

That was all I needed. I pushed in an inch, the feel of her better than anything I'd ever experienced in my life. It took me a second, but then I realized why it felt so phenomenal. "Baby, are you covered?"

She blinked, trying to focus through the haze of that first orgasm. "Huh?"

"Birth control. You say the word and I'll put on a condom. But if it's okay with you, I want to feel you bare. Nothing between us."

Her throat bobbed as she swallowed. "I-I'm on birth control."

I nearly drove all the way into her at that declaration but fisted the comforter where my hands were braced in the mattress on either side of her head. "And you're okay with it?"

She traced my lips with her finger as her eyes locked with mine. "I don't want there to be anything between us."

I pushed into her on a smooth glide, hissing through gritted teeth at how exquisite she felt when I bottomed out.

"Tristan," she cried out, arching her back off the bed and digging her nails into my back.

"Feels like heaven," I grunted, pulling out and driving back in, each thrust harder than the last. Her body was sheer perfection, and I knew, as I stared down into her eyes, getting lost in the sea green, I would never get enough. She was it for me. I loved her. Whether or not she was ready to hear it didn't make it any less true. I was in love with her. And I knew I would be until I took my very last breath.

As the room filled with her sweet sounds and sweat

beaded between our bodies, I felt her walls flutter around me, and I knew she was getting close.

"Let go, Dandelion," I grunted, my molars clenched tight to keep from coming before her.

Her eyes flared. "It—It's too much."

"It's not. I'm right here. I've got you. Just trust me."

Her body locked tight beneath mine, and she splintered into a million pieces. Crying out my name as she came. I rode it out for as long as I possibly could until the squeeze of her pussy became too much, then I buried my face in her neck and followed her over that edge into the abyss.

As we came down, and a sated smile curved her lips, those three little words were on the tip of my tongue, and it took everything in me to keep from letting them spill out.

Chapter Twenty-Two

Merritt

"Something's going on. You look all glow-y and happy," Blythe stated, her narrowed gaze studying me from across the table in Evergreen Diner like she could find out all my secrets if she focused hard enough. When she called earlier and asked me to meet with her and a few of her friends for lunch, Tristan insisted he'd watch Levi while I went out, declaring they were going to have "guy time". I had no idea what that entailed, but Levi had been thrilled about the idea, so I said yes.

I was pleasantly surprised when I got to the diner and saw the friends she was having lunch with included Ivy, Rae, and another one of Rhodes's sisters, Holly. She made introductions, and within minutes, it felt like I'd been a part of this crew for years.

I'd met some really incredible women recently, and I looked forward to getting to know each of them better. Warren had been so successful at isolating me from most everyone I cared about that I'd forgotten what it felt like to have a group of people you could talk to, share all the ups and downs of your life with, and who could lend a shoulder when you needed someone to lean on. I'd been alone for so long, and it had taken some getting used to, but each new friendship I made took one of those jagged pieces of me that had been ripped away and slid it back into place.

"Well, I *am* happy," I told her, a smile stretching across my face at the truth of that. Despite the nasty visit with my brother, a lot had happened recently that ensured my happiness. Warren had been served with divorce papers. Just like with Ozzy, I held out very little hope he would simply sign the papers and go about his life. But I'd prepared for him to do what he could to make it a pain. And that was exactly what he'd done. He hired an attorney of his own who immediately hit back, but Rochelle was a certified badass. She was handling the back and forth, and I trusted her to do right by me so I didn't have to think too much about it. She'd also informed me she was taking on my custody case, and she was going to bury my brother right alongside my soon-to-be ex-husband.

She might have intimidated the hell out of me, but she was officially my favorite person. Well, aside from Levi and Tristan.

"Things are going really good for me right now. I have a good job. Ivy reached out to squeeze my hand at that. "I'm making friends, my attorney has freaking ninja skills, and Levi seems to be doing really well. All of that makes me happy."

Blythe hummed and tapped her chin. "I get all that, and I'm super excited for you, but none of that would explain why you've got that glow."

My brows pinched together. "What glow?"

Rae leaned in and lowered her voice to answer. "The sex glow."

I choked on my iced tea and Blythe pointed in Rae's direction. "Yes, exactly. That's what it is. You have the sex glow."

My cheeks went up in flames, the blush giving me away.

Blythe smacked the table, her jaw hinging open. "Oh my God, you've had sex."

"Shh!" I hissed, looking around to make sure no one was eavesdropping. Yes, I had sex. A lot of sex. And it had been incredible. But I didn't want it broadcasted to the whole diner. Hope Valley's grapevine was not to be taken lightly. All it took was for one person to overhear, and the entire town would know by morning.

I'd learned that after the scene on the sidewalk with Warren and Blythe. That spread through town like wildfire. The restraining order certainly hadn't helped. Word had gotten out that there were pictures of the bruises he'd inflicted, and people were starting to question whether or not he really was the charming, generous man they all thought him to be. That shiny reputation of his was being tarnished, and I would have been lying if I said I didn't get a tiny thrill out of witnessing his fall from grace.

Blythe clasped her hands beneath her chin and shot me a pleading look. "Please tell me you and Tristan are together. That would make me so happy."

"We . . ." We hadn't exactly put a label on what we were doing, but it was the most real thing I'd ever felt. Sure, I had a couple boyfriends in high school, but those had been about childhood infatuation and puppy love. My longest relationship was with Warren, but I never once felt for him what I felt for Tristan. Even when I thought we were good. "I guess you could say we're . . . dating? Seeing each other? I'm not sure of the right term for it."

"It's hard to put a label on it this day and age with how the whole scene has changed," Holly said with understanding. "My niece actually explained it to me not too long ago. Apparently when you're first starting out, it's considered *chatting*. From there, you move onto *talking*."

Rae sipped her lemonade through her straw, her gaze full of curiosity as she asked, "And then you're dating?"

Holly shook her head. "Nope. There's one more level before dating, which is *seeing*. Like you're seeing each other. It's all very specific and completely ridiculous."

I reached up to rub at my temples, trying to absorb everything Holly just said. "Well now I'm more confused than ever."

"What all does it entail?" Ivy asked me, popping a grape into her mouth and caressing her belly.

"Obviously sex," Rae specified.

I shot her a look. "Yes, okay. It includes that. It's only been two days, so we haven't had time to go on a date or anything, but there's a lot of touching and kissing, even when sex isn't involved. He cleaned out his closet and dresser and moved all my stuff from the guest room into his the other day. And he converted the garage into a space where I can work on restoring antique furniture because I off-handedly mentioned how much I missed it."

"Oh wow." Holly let out a breath. Rae and Ivy were looking at me with huge grins, and Blythe's hands were clasped over her mouth as her eyes glistened.

Panic clutched at my throat, and for a brief moment, I was worried that she might have changed her mind and didn't want me dating her brother. Or *seeing* him, or whatever the word for it was. "Are you crying?"

She began to wave her hands in front of her face frantically. "No! Maybe. Okay, yes, but they're good tears. I thought maybe you and Tristan were enjoying time together and maybe hooking up. But what you described, it's . . ."

"It's what?" I asked when she trailed off.

"It sounds an awful lot like love," Ivy answered, and the fork I'd been holding clattered onto my plate.

"What?" I squeaked. "No. No way! He doesn't—it isn't—it's not *that*. We just really like each other."

Rae cocked her head to the side as she watched me. "Are you denying it because you don't think it's true, or because you don't want it to be true?"

"I—" My mouth suddenly felt dry as the desert. "It's too soon," I said softly, my voice going small as that stupid voice in the back of my head piped up. She always had the worst timing, and I was really starting to hate her. "What if . . . what if this goes bad too?" My deepest, most shameful feelings bubbled up from the surface, threatening to choke me if I didn't get them out. "What if it's me that's the problem?"

Blythe's hands came across the table and grabbed hold of mine. "Stop that. You can't think like that. There is nothing wrong with you."

That voice was relentless. "That can't be true. The two most important men in my life turned out to be the worst kinds of human beings."

"That is not on you," Rae said fiercely, her beautiful face pulling into a scowl.

"I'm not saying I made them into what they are, but what does it say about me that I stuck by my brother for so long? Year after year, making excuses for him when, deep down, I knew what he really was. What does it say about me that I believed Warren when he said he was sorry and swore he would never hurt me again?"

Blythe's fingers tightened around mine. "You see those as flaws, but what I see is a woman with an amazing capacity to love and forgive."

"To my own detriment. Some people would consider that naïve and gullible."

"You were, what? Twenty-one when you met Warren?" Ivy asked. "You were barely an adult. You'd just lost your mother, who you loved dearly, and were alone in the world for the first time. Give yourself a little grace, honey."

Rae picked up where Ivy left off. "Ozzy was the only family you had left. It's not out of the realm of possibility that you'd want to hold on to that relationship. You spent your whole life loving him, and he wasn't always what he is now, right?"

I nodded, a knot forming in my throat. "Right."

"Then you need to forgive yourself for being human," Blythe asserted. "Forgive yourself for not doing the best thing right out of the gate, because there isn't a person on this planet who gets everything correct the first time around. We learn and we grow. That's what you're doing right now. You learned from those experiences, and you used them to make you stronger. You know what you want now, what you deserve, and you're learning to demand exactly that."

Her words penetrated, sinking deep beneath my skin and burying themselves into my soul. They took root and shot out, spreading through me and filling every small, dark corner that Warren's and Ozzy's cruelty had left behind. Those words filled me up and snuffed out that voice inside my head that kept trying to pull me back down and fill me with doubt at every turn.

This was what friends did. They held you up when you needed a little help staying on your feet. They were there to strangle out that self-doubt and insecurity. They were the ones who built you back up when you'd been torn down to nothing.

That was why Warren didn't want me to have anyone around but him. Because if I'd had friends like these when we'd been together, they would have kept me strong and been right there to repair the damage he inflicted, mentally and physically.

What I realized in that very moment was I hadn't lost that inner strength. It hadn't disappeared or been ripped away from me like I thought. Warren didn't succeed in stealing it. It had been there all along. I'd needed a little time to find it again. And now that I had, I wasn't going to let anyone try to take it from me.

I lifted my gaze to Blythe's and said the words I'd been thinking for months. "I know you might not believe it, but you saved me that day."

Her chin jerked back in surprise, and I knew she knew exactly what day I was referring to. The day she finally helped me find the courage to get out.

"I didn't—"

I shook my head to silence her. "You might not think you did anything, but you'd be wrong. I know I would have found a way to save myself one day, but you made me feel brave enough that day to take the first step, because I knew you'd be right there with me. I guess what I'm trying to say is, thank you. Thank you for being my friend then, and thank you for being my friend now."

Blythe sniffled, her eyes growing glassy before she cleared her throat and shook her head. "So help me God, Merritt, if you make me cry right now, I'm going to be seriously pissed."

Everyone at the table burst into laughter. Including me.

Chapter Twenty-Three

Merritt

I was nervous. My belly felt like it was full of so many butterflies, it was a wonder I hadn't floated away.

As Tristan guided the Suburban up the gravel path, he and Levi chattered along like it was any other day, oblivious to the fact that I was sitting in the passenger seat, freaking the hell out.

Blythe's house came into view a second later, but I was so in my head I barely had it in me to appreciate how beautiful her home was and how tranquil the wooded area surrounding it felt. It was like being in a world all your own while still being close enough to civilization for anything else you could possibly need.

Tristan's hand covered mine and his thumb gently

worked my fingers apart. "You have nothing to be nervous about."

Apparently he wasn't as oblivious as I thought. Not that I should have been surprised.

"That's easy for you to say," I grumped as he pulled between Blythe's car and a big truck I didn't recognize and shifted into park. "You know everyone here already."

He twisted in his seat to face me. "You know Blythe. Hell, you two are practically besties."

That was true. But it wasn't Blythe I was concerned about. Tonight was the night I met Tristan's parents, and after discussing at length—more than once, since I kept changing my mind—I'd let him convince me to do it as his girlfriend. Making it official and everything. If kids these days had anything to say about it, I was sure they'd tell me we'd jumped past a million levels.

"What if they don't like me?" I asked quietly, giving voice to my biggest fears.

He reached out and pinched my chin between his fingers, gently tipped my face to his. Tristan's expression softened, his eyes tracing tenderly over my features. "They're going to love you," he assured me.

My face pulled into a pout. "You're just saying that."

He smiled, the sight of it melting my insides. "I'm not. It's the truth, Dandelion. Think about it. They raised me and Blythe, they had a hand in molding us into the people we are. So it wouldn't really be a stretch to think they might like a person their son and daughter both liked, don't you think?"

"I think you're the coolest, Aunt Merri," Levi announced from the back.

I twisted around and smiled at him. "Thanks for that, little dude. It makes me feel a lot better."

"No problem. Hey, Tristan. Do you know if there are gonna be vegetables tonight? 'Cause I'm *really* tired of vegetables."

Tristan laughed, and I shot him a threatening look. Needless to say, the battle over vegetables was still raging strong in our house, neither of us willing to back down. I was determined to make sure Levi had a healthy, well-rounded diet, and Levi was determined to turn my hair gray by bitching relentlessly.

Before we could get into it for the millionth time, the front door of Blythe's house was thrown open, and a striking older woman with the most beautiful red hair stepped across the threshold onto the front porch. She waved excitedly and bounced in place.

Tristan let out a huff of annoyance. "I told my mom to play it cool. Should've known she wouldn't be able to help herself."

"That's your mom?"

"Yep. And if you can't tell by looking at her, she's a little excited to meet you and Levi."

"Of course she is," Levi said like it was just common sense. "We're the awesome-est. I have, like, a bazillion friends who'll say so."

My nephew's confidence was certainly something to strive for, that was for sure.

"We should get in there. If we leave her standin' there much longer, her head might explode."

I let out a breath and steeled my spine. Pushing the door open, I climbed out of the car and cast the woman on the porch a wobbly smile as I returned her wave. Tristan rounded the hood and took my hand, and I did my best not to look like I was walking to the gallows as we closed the distance and climbed the steps.

"Hi. I'm—" That was all I got out before she lunged, wrapping me in a bone-crushing hug and swaying side to side.

"I know who you are. I'm Nona, and it's so wonderful to finally meet you." She released me and cupped my cheeks in her hands, smiling at me with huge, happy, teal blue eyes that matched Blythe's. "My son's told me so much. You're even more beautiful than he described."

Tristan groaned from behind me. "Mom, we talked about this. You promised you'd be cool, remember?"

She shot her son a glare. "I'm being very cool. You've never appreciated how cool I am."

A small giggle escaped my lips as mother and son scowled at each other.

It was Levi who broke the standoff, saying, "My aunt's cool too. That's what I was just tellin' her in the car, 'cause she was super nervous to see you."

My cheeks caught fire, and I would have given anything to have a piece of tape to slap over his adorable, unfiltered little mouth.

Nona's scowl fell away, and her smile was full of warmth and acceptance. "Well, I'm glad she has you to set her straight when she starts thinking silly thoughts," she told Levi. "It's a very important job, reminding people how awesome they are whenever they're feeling a little down or something, and I bet you're really good at it."

My nephew's chest swelled up. "I do it all the time with my friends. When Tommy struck out in kickball the other day and started sayin' he was no good, I reminded him last week he kicked the ball so hard it went over the fence and into the road. That made him feel better, and on his next turn, he got a homerun."

Every time I thought it wasn't possible to be any prouder of my nephew, he did something that melted my heart into a puddle. His kindness had no limits or expectations. He gave it freely, without expecting anything in return.

"You've got a very kind heart, Levi."

He nodded earnestly. "Aunt Merri says it don't cost nothin' to be kind, so we should do it every day."

Nona's gaze returned to me, and I swear her eyes took on a sheen in the porch light. "Your aunt is a very wise woman, Levi. You're lucky to have her."

"For sure. We're lucky to have each other."

If he didn't stop being so damn perfect, I was going to start crying. Fortunately, Nona brought the conversation to a close by reaching out her hand to Levi and saying, "My grandkids are really excited to meet you. What do you say we head inside and see what kind of trouble we can get into, huh?"

Levi followed, and I took a moment to sniffle and wave at my eyes to dry the tears that had begun to form.

Tristan used his grip on my hand to tug me into his side, then wrapped his arm around my waist. "Still worried she isn't going to like you?"

I stuck my tongue out at him as we made our way inside. I should have known I had the world's best nephew at my back to hype me up whenever I needed it.

I COULDN'T REMEMBER the last time I'd had so much fun. By the time we'd finished the amazing dinner Blythe prepared—where there *were* vegetables, much to Levi's chagrin—and were sitting around the dining table with coffee as we let our dessert settle, I was bordering on uncomfortably full—the chocolate cake Nona brought was the best I'd ever eaten— yet still feeling light as air.

The muscles in my abs had gotten a workout from how much and how hard I'd laughed all evening. It hadn't taken long at all for me to grow comfortable with Trick and Nona. I should have realized that a man as wonderful as Tristan could only have been raised by parents just as amazing.

The ease in which they had accepted Levi and me into their fold, like it was as natural as breathing, slotted a few more of those jagged pieces into place until I was nearly whole. After the years with Warren, I didn't know if it was possible for me to ever feel that way, but there I was.

I'd watched Trick and Nona throughout the evening, and discovered exactly where Tristan's affectionate nature had come from. The love his parents had for each other radiated from them. Even after being married as long as they had, they still looked at each other with stars in their eyes.

Whenever Nona talked, Trick watched her with this small grin on his face that said he still couldn't believe how lucky he was to have her. And whenever he touched Nona, she'd inadvertently lean into it like she couldn't get enough.

Growing up, that was the kind of love I wanted, however after Warren, I'd given up any hope I might have it one day.

But now I was starting to think it might be possible.

"Merritt, honey," Nona said, pulling me from the happy daze of my thoughts and back to the present where the adults were still at the table, enjoying each other's company, and the kids had taken off to go play with Rhodes's dog, Koda. Their constant giggles and intermittent shrieks of delight told us they were having the time of their lives. "Blythe showed me pictures of that sideboard you're restoring for her. It's absolutely breathtaking."

Heat infused my cheeks as a smile overtook my face. I'd been working on that piece whenever I had time—which wasn't as often as I would have liked—and it was coming along better than I could have hoped. I thought for sure I would have been rusty after so many years, but the moment I picked up the sanding block, it all came back to me, and I swear I felt my mother standing right beside me every time I worked on it. I'd been taking pictures of the progress and it felt amazing to have someone admire the work I'd put in so far.

"Thanks. It's been nice to get back to it. I forgot how cathartic it felt to lose myself in the work of bringing something back to life."

Blythe lifted her wine glass to her lips and took a drink. "I'd say you're doing more than that. I looked up pictures online of other pieces from that time period, and what you've done has leveled it up. It still has the original charm, but you've also somehow made it fit perfectly with everything we already have here."

"You could make a very nice living doing what you do," Nona said. "You have a real talent and an obvious passion for it. People would pay an arm and a leg."

I sputtered under her praise. "Oh, no. I don't do it for that. I'm not looking to make money. I like doing it. It's not like I'm charging or anything."

"You should," Tristan added, turning to look at me. Like his father, he'd spent most of the evening finding little ways to touch or caress me, to let me know he was there and to show he cared. Just then, his arm was draped over the back of my chair, alternating between twirling strands of my hair around his fingers and gently brushing the pads across the nape of my neck. "This is something you love doing, and you're great at it. You should go for it." He gave me a crooked grin. "I'll even be your first customer."

"Uh, not gonna happen, little bro," Blythe cut in, then raised her eyebrows at me. "She's already working on something for me, and I fully intend on paying her for what she's done. Whether she likes it or not."

"You don't have to do that."

"Yes, I do. Know your worth, babe. And know the worth of your work."

God, she really was the best friend a woman could ask for. I wondered, not for the first time, how I'd gotten so lucky.

We left not long after, when it became clear that Levi was fading fast. We said our goodbyes, and I found I was actually looking forward to the next family dinner. Tristan's entire family was amazing. We'd barely turned off the gravel lane that led up to Rhodes and Blythe's house before Levi was out cold in his booster seat.

"You have fun tonight, Dandelion?" Tristan asked, taking my hand in his and lifting it to his lips to kiss my knuckles as he steered with the other one.

"I had the best time. Your family is incredible."

He shot me a happy smile before looking back at the

dark road ahead. "I'm glad. And they loved you. So maybe next time, you won't have to be so nervous."

We lapsed into a calm, comfortable silence as we headed for home that lasted until I had a thought.

"Tristan?"

"Yeah, baby?"

"You were right."

He quirked a brow my way. "About what?"

"Doc is a far superior dog."

He barked out a laugh and squeezed my hand tighter. "Damn right he is. And the fact that you see it means you're perfect for me."

Chapter Twenty-Four

Merritt

By the time my shift at the lodge was over, my feet were tired and there was a constant ache in my lower back, but I didn't mind. Being tired and sore meant I'd done a good day's work, and I honestly didn't mind cleaning rooms.

Levi's social worker had been impressed with how well he was doing after such a traumatic experience, and even offered to testify on my behalf in my custody case if it came to that.

We'd been living with Tristan for about three months now, and each day was better than the one before. We'd fallen into a routine unlike anything I'd experienced. It was safe and comfortable. It felt like we were our own little family, complete with a small dog with a big personality. I was finally where I was always meant to be. I knew in my heart this was the happy life my mother had told me to go out and find before she passed away, and I had no doubt she was looking down on Levi and me and smiling.

"You finally off?" Becky asked as I hit the bottom of the stairs.

"Yep. I think tonight calls for an Epsom salt bath and a glass of wine." I reached into my purse and fished out my keys.

"You deserve it, honey. You've been workin' hard."

Ivy was getting closer to her due date, and though she fought her boyfriend on it tooth and nail, she'd finally relented to taking six weeks off once the baby was born. When Ivy asked if I'd be interested in handling some of the work she did for the resort, I'd been honored she trusted me enough and said yes without a second thought. So on top of my regular work, I was also training to take over for her so she could actually relax on her maternity leave and not worry that things here were going to hell.

It was a lot, and most days I felt like there was so much information in my head there couldn't possibly be room for more, but I was excited for the challenge.

I walked backward, grinning in her direction as I began, "You know what they say . . . it's not work if you love what you're doing," we both said at the same time. It was a mantra Becky lived by and said at least once every day.

"Look at you, catching on quick." She shot me a wink. "You enjoy your evening with that gorgeous man and that adorable little boy."

Word of my relationship had spread through the lodge after Tristan and Levi surprised me at work one day a few weeks back. They had made a special lunch they wanted to bring me, and we'd eaten it together at one of the picnic tables outside. Tristan hadn't shied away from touching me while they'd hung out during my break, and when they got ready to leave, he'd given me a kiss right out front for everyone to see. Fortunately, it was G-rated, considering there were kids and families running around everywhere, but it still set tongues wagging.

It was the same in town. The cat was out of the bag after that first family dinner a couple months back. It seemed like everyone in town knew. Even people I'd never spoken to. There had been a couple days where I panicked, worried what Warren would do when he found out. Because in a town like Hope Valley, it was a foregone conclusion it was *when*, not *if*. Tristan had to talk me out of spiraling a couple of times, but I'd eventually settled.

The divorce proceedings were moving at a snail's

pace, and as badly as I wanted them over with, I trusted Rochelle when she said this was the way things went. When it came to divorces and the like, there was a whole lot of what she called "hurry up and wait." It sucked, but I wasn't going to let it cast a shadow on my life. Not when it was finally so bright and sunny.

"I will, Becky. You have a good night too."

I headed out of the lodge and rounded the back where the staff parked, waving goodbye to different people—staff and guests alike—as I passed them. Pressing the button on the remote, I beeped the locks once I was a few feet away from my car, and pulled the door open, tossing my purse across to the passenger seat. I was just about to climb in when a flash of red out of the corner of my eye caught my attention.

I slowly turned my head, a chill working its way down my spine as soon as I spotted the flowers propped up where the hood met the windshield. The blood in my veins turned to ice at the sight of those six, perfect, long-stem red roses. It wasn't the flowers themselves that scared me.

It was what they represented and who they were from that did.

Those were the very flowers Warren would bring me as an apology every time he hit me. I'd received so many bouquets of red roses, that the sight and smell of them made me sick to my stomach. I hated roses now, and he knew that.

Just like I knew they weren't currently resting on the hood of my car because Warren was sorry about anything. They were meant to scare me.

Unfortunately for him, his little plan didn't work. I was done letting him intimidate and threaten me. I was done letting him control me with fear.

I spun around, looking in every direction to see if I could spot him, even though my gut was telling me he was long gone.

"You sick, manipulative bastard," I said on a growl. I snatched up the bouquet and beat it against the hood. The flowers exploded, raining torn and tattered petals all over the place, but I didn't stop until all I was holding were six scraggly twigs. Just in case he *was* still around and was watching, I wanted him to see I wasn't scared of him. I was pissed.

I was in the middle of stomping the stems and grinding them into the dirt as I let out a string of curses that would have made a whole boatload of sailors blush when the sound of a throat clearing broke through my haze of rage.

I looked up to find Raylan Bradbury, Rhodes's brother and the excursion guide for the resort, watching me like I'd lost my ever-loving mind. "Those roses do somethin' to piss you off?"

I blew at the hair that had fallen into my face and tried to catch my breath as I struggled to get control of myself. "Uh . . . h-hi."

His brows winged up toward his hairline. "You okay, Merritt? You need me to call Tristan for you or anything?"

"No. I mean, yeah. I'm fine." I pushed my hair back, my fingers catching on a tangle from the little jig I'd just danced on those rose stems. My tongue poked out to wet my suddenly dry lips. "Um . . . did you happen to see someone sneaking around out here who looked out of place?"

His expression changed from humorous to serious. "What's goin' on, Mer? Did something happen?"

I curled my lips between my teeth. "Well. Kind of. But it really isn't a big deal. It's just . . . I think Warren was here."

In the blink of an eye, his jaw tensed and he stiffened like he was on alert. "He what?"

"Really, there's no reason to make this a thing. I'm pretty sure he's already gone, anyway."

"What's going on?"

God! Was everyone and their dog coming through here right now?

I looked over my shoulder as Lennix came up to join us. "Nothing," I answered at the same time Raylan said, "Her fucker ex was here, lurkin' around."

Lennix's eyes bugged out so wide I worried they were going to fall out of her skull. "Are you serious?" she practically shrieked.

"Len, why don't you rein in the screamin' before you bust someone's ear drum and get Merritt inside where it's safe while I take a look around to see if he's still here."

The attitude Raylan just shot her way had me sucking in a gasp. Lennix threw him a glare so vicious I was shocked it didn't melt the skin off his face, but she did it while hooking her arm through mine and giving me a little tug.

"And how about, while you're out here looking, you see if you can locate that stick that's been shoved up your ass and yank it out?" she snapped. Before he had a chance to rebut, she jerked me around and pulled me toward the lodge.

I chanced a glance over my shoulder and saw Raylan still standing there, watching as she stormed away. Competing expressions of anger and torment tore across his face before he shook himself out of it and took off in the opposite direction.

"Um, Len, sweetie, are you okay?"

She muttered a string of curses under her breath as we clomped up the steps of the lodge's back deck. With her free hand, she pulled her cell from her back pocket and dragged her thumb across the screen, typing out something with that one digit with more skill than I had using both hands to text. The message she composed whooshed off, and she stuffed it back into her pocket before turning to me with a sympathetic smile. "Yeah, I'm good. He's an asshole, don't think about it for another second."

The moment we hit the lobby, Ivy and Becky were there, crowding around us. "Oh my God. Merritt, are you okay?" Ivy's words came out in a rush. I knew without having to ask who Lennix had been texting a second ago, and I had a feeling I was about to have a lot more company.

Sure enough, Lennix's text had gone around like a game of telephone, and within a matter of minutes, Rae, her husband, Zach, and Zach's parents, Rory and Cord, had gathered in the lobby at the lodge. Ten minutes later, Tristan came blasting through the door like a hurricane, his gorgeous face twisted up with fury and concern.

He didn't stop until the tips of his shoes touched mine. He reached up and took my face in both his hands, bringing his forehead to mine, and inhaled like it was the first full one he'd taken in the past several minutes.

He held me like that for several seconds, like he needed to feel me to reassure himself I was here and I was okay before pulling back and scanning me up and down. He still hadn't let me go as his eyes traced every single inch of me.

I wrapped my fingers around his wrists and pulled his hands from my face so I could twine our fingers together. "I'm fine. I swear."

Zach spoke up then. The angry expression on his face was one I'd seen him wear frequently, but Rae had informed me it was all for show. He played at being grumpy, but really, he was as soft as fluff on the inside.

"Rest assured, this is never gonna happen again. I'm callin' Rhodes tomorrow and havin' security cameras installed around the property."

My eyes widened. "You really don't have to do that." I was sure something like that cost a pretty penny, and I hated the thought of him shelling it out because of me.

His face softened. "Should've done it a long time ago, sweetheart. It's for the best, really. It'll make sure you're safe from that asshole, and it's also another level of security for our guests. It's a win-win."

I wasn't sure I believed him, but the stubborn set of his jaw told me he wasn't going to be deterred. "Fine. As long as it isn't *just* because of me. I mean, I didn't see him. I don't know when he was here."

Tristan's thumbs swiped back and forth across the pulse points in my wrists, pulling my focus back to him. "What makes you certain he was here?"

I huffed out a breath. "He left flowers on my car."

Tristan's brows pulled together. "Flowers? And you're sure it was him?"

I nodded, pulling my bottom lip between my teeth and biting down nervously because I knew Tristan was *not* going to like what I said next. "I'm sure. It was six long-stemmed red roses. Those were his apology flowers. He gave them to me every time he hit me."

Sure enough, Tristan's expression turned murderous. His cheeks grew ruddy and the vein in his temple began to throb. A haze moved over his eyes, and I knew he wasn't with me anymore. He was somewhere else, lost in his anger.

I'd never seen that look on him before, and if this had been a few months earlier, it might have scared the hell out of me. But now I knew Tristan would never hurt me. He might have looked like he was seconds away from morphing into the Incredible Hulk, but there wasn't a single part of me that feared what he might do.

"Hey. Come back to me." I placed my hands on the

sides of his neck and forced him to lean in closer to my level. "I'm right here. You need to come back."

He blinked, and just like that, my Tristan was standing in front of me once again. "Dandelion." That word came out in a rasp.

"Whatever he planned on those flowers doing didn't work. I'm right here, and I'm fine, so you need to be too. Okay? He doesn't get a second of our energy."

Tristan's chest rose on a controlled inhale. He closed his eyes, and his lips moved wordlessly as he counted to ten before giving those baby blues back to me. "What do you want to do? You want to go to the station and file a report?"

"I want to go home," I answered without hesitation.

"Baby—"

"I stomped those flowers to death in a fit of rage."

"She did," Raylan confirmed. "Walked up on her grinding them to dust under her shoe and cussin' up a storm that'd put the devil to shame."

The corner of Tristan's mouth trembled in a barely-suppressed grin at that news. "Would've paid to see that."

I rolled my eyes. "Yeah, well, it wasn't one of my finest moments. Though, I'd say I was entitled. But there's no point in reporting this. As far as I'm concerned, Warren's the only one who suffered anything from this little stunt."

Tristan's expression turned bewildered. "How do you figure that?"

A sly grin curled my lips up. "Because he wasted money on expensive flowers that I destroyed in two seconds flat. And when I get home, I'm going to forget all about this."

Pride flashed across Tristan's features right before he brought his lips down on mine. "So goddamn strong," he said under his breath.

And he was right. I was strong. And that son of a bitch did not get to win.

Chapter Twenty-Five

Tristan

I'd watched Merritt like a hawk since we got home from the lodge the evening before, waiting to see if there would be a delayed reaction to the stunt that piece of shit had pulled, wanting to be there if the nightmares reared their ugly heads, but nothing happened.

She went about the rest of the night like she did every other night. She made dinner and chatted about all the things happening at the lodge. She asked Levi about his day, and listened raptly as he shared his latest adventures.

I paced the kitchen while she was upstairs, getting the little guy ready for bed, and after she'd tucked him in, she came back down to me and had a glass of wine like we did every night. She'd slept peacefully in my arms all night long, not a nightmare to be found. And I knew that because I hadn't been able to sleep, too busy waiting for the other shoe to drop. It still hadn't by the time the sun rose on a new day.

Ivy had insisted she take the day off, and if Merritt was going to be home, I was too. Even if she was okay, I couldn't seem to get a handle on my emotions. I felt like I was coming out of my skin, and the only thing that helped at all was being near her so I could make sure she was safe. I didn't trust anyone else to do it. So instead of going into the station, I'd spent the morning pouring over the files on Harrison's and my drug case from the comfort of the dining room while Merritt worked on another antique piece in the garage. The only noise in the house—aside from Doc's rattling snore—was the faint strains of the music Merritt was playing in the garage as she worked.

We still hadn't gotten anywhere on the case, and with every day that passed without a lead, the more frustrated Harrison and I became. Ozzy had stopped talking completely, refusing to see either of us if we went to the prison. As bad as it sounded, without another victim, we were stalled, with nowhere to go.

Letting out a frustrated sigh, I pushed the file away and pinched the bridge of my nose. The muscles in my shoulders and back had started to ache, and when I looked at the clock on the microwave, I discovered it was because I'd been sitting in the same position for hours. The legs of the chair creaked as I pushed back from the table and stood.

Merritt tended to lose track of time when she was immersed in a restoration project. It wasn't unheard of for her to go a whole day without eating and not realize it, so instead of letting that magnetic pull between us carry me into the garage, I made my way into the kitchen and opened the fridge, scanning everything inside, hoping to get an idea of what to make her for lunch.

When I'd been content in my bachelor lifestyle, my fridge and cupboards were usually running low. I mainly survived on takeout and whatever Blythe cooked and froze for me whenever she took pity on me or worried about my poor eating habits. But since she and Levi moved in, the fridge and pantry were always stocked, and I certainly didn't miss the days when I'd pull it open to find a single bottle of mustard and a carton of expired milk.

That wasn't the only change in this house over the past few months, and as I gave myself time to take it all in, I realized everything she or Levi had done had been an improvement. Their personalities were tucked into every corner, from whatever book Merritt was currently reading sitting on the coffee table, to her favorite throw blanket tossed over the back of the couch so she could wrap it around her the next time she sat down.

I had throw pillows and framed pictures scattered about now. Merritt has taken precious memories we'd made together and printed them so we could see them every time we walked by. There was a picture of Levi and Doc on the bookshelf behind the couch. One of Merritt with her little guy sitting on the porch swing at Blythe's, eating ice cream cones, sat on a side table. She'd printed out a selfie I took of the three of us the day we let Levi talk us into dressing up like wrestlers, using nothing but items we had lying around the house, and displayed it proudly on the mantel. There were pictures of Blythe and her family, of my sister and Merritt posing together, of so many incredible moments. But the one on the fireplace would always be my favorite. And I wanted it to stay there forever.

Hell, even the random wrestling figures I found on the floor were better than the cold, boring nothing that had been there before.

They'd come in and breathed life into this house, and I couldn't imagine ever losing it. The thought of them leaving one day made me sick to my stomach. I didn't want things going back to how they'd once been. That was no longer the life I wanted.

My culinary expertise was limited to a few dishes, so

I decided to recreate the first thing she'd ever cooked in this kitchen.

I carried a plate in one hand and a glass of iced tea in the other as I headed for the garage. Merritt stood with her back to me, her hips doing a little shimmy to the song playing from the Bluetooth speaker on the shelf as she took her sanding block after an armoire that had definitely seen better days. When I'd asked what she had planned for the piece of furniture, she didn't know. She'd just known she *had* to buy it when she saw it.

As long as she was passionate about it and it made her happy, she could fill every inch of the house with old, damaged furniture in need of a little TLC.

She was wearing a pair of frayed, faded denim shorts and one of my old T-shirts she'd gathered and tied in a knot at the small of her back, leaving the smallest sliver of skin between the waistband and hem showing. The sight of her in my clothes went straight to my dick, and my erection strained against the fly of my jeans. This was something I could see every day—that I *wanted* to see every day—and never get tired of it.

She spun around when I cleared my throat to announce my presence. She smiled, and like always, the beauty of it stole my breath. It brightened further when she saw what I was holding. She let out a little squeak and hopped in place. "Grilled cheese with tomato?"

I grinned in return. "Is there any other way to eat it?"

She skipped over and took the plate, popping up on the tips of her toes to press a kiss to the corner of my mouth. "Thanks, honey. I didn't realize I was hungry until I saw you holding that sandwich."

I sat the glass down on the workbench and moved closer to inspect the armoire. "How's it going in here?"

"Great," she chirped from around the huge bite she'd taken, her cheeks puffing out like an adorable chipmunk. She swallowed and wiped her mouth with the back of her hand. "I've got a few ideas in my head of what I want to do for this piece, but there's still a lot that needs to be done before I can think about stain or paint."

I took in her expression. The flush of her cheeks and the way her eyes shone. "You really love doing this, huh?"

She shrugged a shoulder. "It's like therapy for me. Puts me at ease."

I moved to her and rested my hands on her hips. It was impossible to be in the same room as her and not touch her. I skimmed my palms to her waist, grinning at the squeak of surprise when I lifted her and sat her down on top of the old dresser she'd been leaning against. The garage was steadily filling up with more furniture she wanted to work on, and it wouldn't be long before she ran out of space, but I'd already been brainstorming ideas on how to remedy that.

I pushed her knees apart and stepped between her thighs, getting as close as possible. "Good, baby. I'm glad it does that for you."

Those fathomless green eyes studied me intensely before she spoke again. "Speaking of being put at ease . . . how can I help you move past what happened yesterday?"

I inhaled deeply, filling my lungs with the scent of orange peels and burnt sugar. I dropped my head into the crook of her neck and relished the way she gently dragged her fingernails up and down the ridges of my spine.

This was all I needed. Just being near her helped to calm the storm inside me.

"You're doin' it. This, right here, is all I need."

She made a humming noise in the back of her throat before tangling her fingers in my hair and using her hold to tilt my head back to meet her eyes. "That's not true, and we both know it. Tristan, you've been watching my every move since we got home yesterday. You might think you're hiding it, but you're wrong. I know you didn't sleep last night because you spent the entire night watching over me."

"I can't help it," I admitted quietly, the words struggling to move past the knot that had formed in my throat. The idea of something happening to you . . ." I clenched my eyes closed, unable to finish that thought.

Her fingers ghosted over my forehead and down my temple in the most soothing touch. "Hey," she whispered. "Look at me."

I forced my eyes open and back to hers. "I know you want to protect me from the world, but you're setting yourself up for failure, honey. Life's unpredictable. There's no way for you to know what the future holds. If you spend all your time focused on what-ifs and worrying about what *could* happen, you're going to miss all the great stuff that's happening right in front of you. I can't stop you from worrying about me, but I want you to know I'm not the same woman I was when we first met. Even if something bad happens to me, I'm strong enough to handle it. I'm strong enough to fight whatever it is and make it back to you."

She was right. I knew that. Just like I knew her strength was unmatched. She was the bravest person I knew, and that bravery was one of the things I loved most about her. But I was still trying to wrap my brain around all these new feelings she evoked in me.

"This is all so new to me. I've never felt for anyone the way I feel for you. It's so big, so . . . important, that sometimes it feels like it could consume me if I let it."

She breathed deeply, her throat bobbing on a swallow. "I know the feeling," she admitted softly.

"You and Levi came into my life and threw it into the most perfect, most exciting chaos, and lately, I've struggled with the thought of you guys leaving, and taking all of that with you. And I keep thinking, I don't want to go back to how my life was before you guys were in it."

She pulled in a sharp breath, but I wasn't done. "It was impossible not to fall in love with you, Dandelion. I didn't bother trying to stop it."

Her lips formed an O. The green in her eyes darkened, her pupils expanding as the depth of what I said hit her.

"You . . . you love me?"

"I've been holding those words in for a really long time because I didn't want to scare you off. And it's okay if you aren't ready to say them back. I had to tell you the truth. I love you, Merritt. You and Levi both. I know none of this was supposed to be forever, that it was a temporary fix to an unexpected situation. But I'm going to ask you to consider making it forever. I don't want you to go. I want this to be your home."

"Tristan," she whispered, that one word so full of emotion.

"You want to know how you can help me move past

yesterday? Give me your tomorrow and every day after that. Knowing you're mine is all I need."

"Tristan. You have me." She said those words with such reverence I felt them down to my very soul. "For as long as you want me, I'm yours, because I love you too. I'm not going anywhere."

Just like that, the vise that had been squeezing around my chest since the night before released.

She loved me. *Christ*, hearing her say that was the best feeling in the whole world. She loved me.

Leaning in, I brushed my lips against hers as hunger and need exploded inside me. "Need you, Merritt," I growled against her lips. "Right now. I can't wait."

Her tongue came out and ran across my bottom lip. "Then don't."

Chapter Twenty-Six

Merritt

Tristan's mouth slammed down on mine, pouring every ounce of his desire for me into the kiss. It was hungry and desperate and so full of need it made my skin vibrate.

"Tristan," I panted, pulling in a breath when he ripped his mouth from mine to drag his lips and teeth down my neck and along my collarbone. My hands came up and tangled in his hair, holding him to me. It was the only way I could think to stay grounded as he worked the button of my shorts open and slid his hand inside.

A whimper pushed past my lips at the first swipe of his fingers through my wetness.

He pulled back, the blue of his eyes swallowed by his dilated pupils. "Already ready for me."

"This is what you always do to me. I can't get

enough of you touching me." My words ended on a cry as he slid his fingers past my folds and deep inside me. Words left me completely when he crooked them in a come-hither motion, rubbing against a place inside me that had never been touched before.

"Oh God!" I cried, my body jolting at the sensation. It felt like I was levitating right off the dresser. "So good. Never been like this." My sentences came out choppy and incomplete as my body strung tighter, making it impossible to form a coherent thought.

"Jesus," Tristan grunted against my throat, his tongue flicking over my pulse. "The way your body responds to me, Dandelion. I can feel you getting close."

His thumb came into play then, pressing down against my clit as he brushed that place inside, and every single cell in my body, every nerve ending and neuron, exploded outward into the atmosphere.

"Christ, you're so fuckin' pretty when you come," he murmured against my lips as he slipped his hand from my shorts. A tremor worked through my body as I watched him bring his glistening fingers to his lips and lick them clean of my arousal. "Sweetest thing I've ever tasted."

I'd come so hard I couldn't think straight, but seeing how his eyes flared at the taste of me, the way his desire for me was carved into every line and angle of his face made me want him all over again.

"Please," I begged, needing more. Needing *everything*.

"Please what, baby? What are you asking for?"

I went from pleading to demanding in the blink of an eye. "I need you inside me. *Now*, Tristan." Fisting the material of his shirt, I whipped it up and over his head, tossing it aside. We tore at each other's clothes until we were both naked in only a few seconds.

Tristan grabbed me by the waist and spun me around so fast my hair whipped into my face. "Want you like this," he said, pressing his chest against my back, forcing me to lean forward and brace my hands on the top of the dresser. He moved behind me, his thick, long cock slipping between my legs from behind and dragging through my slit. His hand caressed every inch of my body that he could reach as he dragged his teeth along the crook of my shoulder.

His tip nudged against my entrance, and I sucked in a bracing breath, preparing myself to take him, but he didn't push in right away.

When he stayed motionless, I turned to look back at him over my shoulder.

"Is this okay?" he asked, needing to know I wanted everything he was doing before taking it any further. He was always taking care of me. It was one of the many, *many* things I loved, that made him so damn special.

"More than okay. I need to feel you."

He entered me in one swift thrust, his hips snapping against my ass as he buried himself deep, stretching me wide. No matter how many times we'd done this, that first thrust still drove the air from my lungs. He was so much bigger than anyone who had come before.

"Oh God," I groaned, dropping my head forward and pressing my hands harder into the scarred wood of the dresser. "You're so deep like this."

"Fuck, you feel like heaven wrapped around me," he panted as he pulled out and drove back it.

"It's never been like this," I confessed as I began to rock my hips, pushing back into him every time he slammed forward. "Never been this good."

I felt his mouth at my neck, kissing and sucking the skin there as he lost control and fucked me harder . . . faster. "You were made for me. Merritt. Made to be mine. Say it, baby. Tell me you're mine."

I didn't hesitate. "I'm yours," I breathed as the tension in my core started to build again. "I'm yours, Tristan."

"Goddamn right you are," he grunted. "Now come for me, baby," he ordered, tipping his hips in a way that hit my G-spot at the same time he reached down to where we were connected and began circling my clit.

I shattered into a million pieces, bursting apart like the stars behind my eyes. My whole world lit up in technicolor. His name was a benediction on my lips as I came harder than I ever had before.

"Love you," he growled against my ear before burying himself deep and following me over the edge into sheer bliss.

Tristan's fingers trailed along my back in slow, lazy movements, brushing up and down along the ridges of my spine. The touch was calming, soothing, and added to the peace of the moment. These were my favorites times of day. The minutes that came after we made love, when Tristan and I were lying in bed wrapped around each other. In those minutes, nothing existed but the two of us. We got to exist in our own peaceful little bubble for a short period of time before the rest of the world came creeping back in.

He must have enjoyed these moments as much as I did, because as soon as he came down from his release, he didn't bother putting on a single stitch of clothing before he scooped me up into his arms and carried me through the house to *our* bedroom, where he proceeded to lock us in an intimate embrace.

I snuggled deeper into his chest, his arm wrapped around my waist tightened, pulling me against him. My mind blinked back to the conversation we'd had right before we went at each other like animals. He loved me.

The thought made me giddy with joy. The smile that stretched across my face was so big it made my cheeks hurt. He loved me, and he wanted Levi and me to stay with him for good.

His voice came out low and raspy as he said, "I feel you smiling against my skin, Dandelion. What's got you grinning so big?"

I didn't bother schooling my features as I folded my hands on top of his chest and braced my chin on top so I could look at his gorgeous face. He looked as relaxed as I felt. His lids were heavy over those sky-blue eyes. The contentment etched into the planes of his face looked incredible on him. He was so beautiful.

"You love me."

"I do," he confirmed.

"That's why I'm smiling." My smile got impossibly bigger, but happiness drowned out the throb in my cheeks at the stretch.

The grin Tristan returned warmed me from the

inside out. "I take it from the Joker grin that you liked hearin' that."

I gave his chest a smack then reached to twist his nipple in retaliation for his teasing.

"Ah, Christ! I was just jokin'!" He reached up to rub the abused skin, his bottom lip sticking out in a pout as he scowled down at me. "Rude."

"You deserved it for making fun of me." My sentence ended on a squeal when Tristan sprang into action, changing our position so fast my hair flew into my eyes. He used his hips to pin me to the mattress, hovering over me and reaching up to brush the hair back from my face.

"I love you," he rasped, the playfulness gone from his expression and replaced with utter sincerity.

"I love you too," I returned softly. Joy swelled inside of me, growing so big I worried my skin wouldn't be able to contain it all, and it would come bursting from the tips of my toes and fingers like beams of light. "So much, Tristan."

A rumbling sound roiled through his chest as he gave me more of his weight. "Christ. I'll never get tired of hearin' that. Say it again, baby," he requested.

"I love you." My lips brushed against his as I gave him those words. I felt him start to grow hard again, but just as he was leaning in to kiss me, a sharp, demanding bark rose from the floor beside the bed.

Tristan dropped his forehead into the crook of my shoulder and let out a pained groan. "Cockblockin' little shit," he muttered under his breath, making me laugh.

As though Doc heard him and wanted to make his displeasure at the name calling known, he barked again, this time tacking a small, pathetic growl onto the end.

"He probably just needs to go out," I said on a giggle.

Tristan lifted his head and shot him a glare. "You have a doggie door, for Christ's sake. Why won't you ever use it?"

"For the same reason he feels he should be carted around all day instead of walking," I answered drolly, shooting him an accusatory expression. "Because you've spoiled him rotten."

He didn't have a rebuttal for that. He knew I was right. Doc barked again, as if to agree with me.

Tristan pushed up with a groan, sitting up and throwing his legs over the side of the bed. "Fine," he grumbled, making his way over to the dresser and pulling out a pair of navy boxer briefs since the clothes we'd stripped off earlier were still in a pile in the garage.

Without him curled up in the bed with me, I had no desire to stay there, so I got up as well, throwing on another one of his T-shirts and padding down the hall after him. As he let Doc out, I caught sight of the files and documents he'd been working on earlier. They were strewn across the table like he'd gotten frustrated at something and shoved them away. Instinct had me moving in that direction, my fingers itching to reorganize and straighten up. A hazard of my current job I'd started bringing home with me lately, I guess.

I picked up a couple papers and tapped the edges against the table to stack them together neatly, then put them aside. I flipped the top of a folder closed and spotted a photo underneath.

Picking it up, I flipped it around to face Tristan and asked, "Why do you have a picture of Walter Reeves?"

Tristan's eyes bounced from the man in the printed-out driver's license photo to me. "He was one of the overdose vics in the same drug case your brother's wrapped up in."

I knew about that case. He'd come home grumpy and frustrated more than once because they weren't getting anywhere.

His brows pulled together. "You know him?"

"Not personally. He was part of Warren's inner circle so I saw him around, occasionally talked to him, but that's it. I never really liked him," I admitted. "He was creepy and chauvinistic, as were all those other guys he's friends with."

Something shifted over Tristan's expression, and he started riffling through the documents. He pulled out five more photographs and put them in a line on the table. "Do you recognize any of these people?"

I frowned up at Tristan. "These are all the people who overdosed?"

He nodded gravely, and I knew by the look on his face that this case was still bothering him. I studied the photographs and pointed at one on the far left. "This guy looks familiar." I sifted through my mind, trying to recall where I knew him from. "I think it was at a charity banquet Warren took me to. I was coming back from the bathroom and saw them over in a corner by the bar. It looked like they were arguing about something."

"You don't know what?"

I shook my head. "Warren never really shared much about his work with me. I asked, but he told me it wasn't any of my business, and I wouldn't be able to understand if he tried to explain it to me."

Tristan let loose a string of curses, calling Warren some incredibly colorful names. "If I ever get the chance to beat that asshole senseless, I won't hesitate."

There was one other face I recognized. He was a guy Warren had gone to college with. Like all of his other friends, I didn't know him well, but I recalled Warren coming home in a bad mood because some kind of business deal between them had fallen through. He was so pissed he'd thrown his dinner plate against the wall and backhanded me across the face. But I didn't share that part of the story with Tristan. He was finally getting over the scene from the day before, and I didn't want him to backslide, not after the perfect afternoon we'd shared.

He studied the documents and photos on the table like he was staring at everything with a fresh set of eyes.

"Did I help with something?" I asked, an ember of hope sparking to life in my gut.

He lifted his gaze to mine and smiled. "You might have, baby. I'll have to look into some things when I go back to work tomorrow, but I think you might have pointed me in a new direction."

I beamed, bouncing in place. "Glad I could help," I chirped.

Tristan wound an arm around my waist and pulled me flush against him. "I'm glad too." He leaned in and nuzzled my neck, spreading goosebumps across my skin. "But I'm done talking about work. There are much more tantalizing ways I want to spend the next couple hours before we have to pick Levi up from school."

With an excited squeal, I broke free from his hold and took off for the bedroom, anticipation heating my blood and core as his footsteps chased after me.

Chapter Twenty-Seven

Merritt

"Some days I want to reach down his throat and rip out his spine with my bare hands."

My hand froze midair, the French fry I'd been bringing to my mouth forgotten at Lennix's passionate—and disturbing—declaration.

It had been a week since Warren left those roses on my car. In that time, Zach had lived up to his promise and put up security cameras around the lodge and at the entrance to the ranch.

There'd been no sign of Warren anywhere, and with no more ominous messages, I assumed he'd gotten the hint he couldn't intimidate me and had decided to move on.

Without him lurking around the corner, life carried on like normal, and my new normal was amazing.

The only thing casting a shadow on all the light in my life was the fact that one of my friends seemed to be struggling.

That argument between Lennix and Raylan the day of the rose incident hadn't been the last tense interaction between them, and people were starting to talk. Mainly Ivy, Rae, Holly, and me. We'd noticed Lennix's sour mood lately and were starting to worry.

That was why I'd decided to head to the Tap Room on my day off to check on her and make sure she was okay. The comment about the spine ripping had been in answer to me asking what was going on between her and Raylan.

I cleared my throat and dropped the fry onto my plate next to the burger I ordered for lunch. "That's . . . vivid."

"I'm sorry." She flopped back in her chair on a huff. "I know I sound a little unhinged."

I shot her a grin. "Just a little."

"He makes me so mad."

I placed my straw between my lips and took a sip of water as I watched my friend closely. "Has it always been like this between you guys?"

She threw her hands up in frustration. "No, that's the thing. I've known him my whole life, and recently he's turned into this raging asshole." Her sigh sounded like it weighed a ton. "He and Zach have been best friends since before I was born, so I grew up with him. I knew we weren't as close as he and my brother were, but I always thought we were friends. Things have been strained since my brother and Rae got married, but it didn't start getting ugly until recently."

Leaning forward, I braced my elbow on the table and rested my chin in my palm. "What happened to make your relationship strained?"

A flush hit her cheeks at my question, and she lowered her head like she was trying to hide behind the curtain of her ebony hair. She curled her lips between her teeth, and I got the distinct impression she hadn't meant to reveal as much as she had.

"Lennix?"

"Ugh! I told him I had feelings for him, okay?" she blurted out in rapid fire, her admission nearly bowling me over.

My eyes went wide and my hand slapped the table as I moved in even closer. "Oh my God, are you serious?" I hissed in part shock, part excitement. "You like Raylan?" All of a sudden I couldn't shake the thought; they would make the cutest couple ever.

"*Liked*," she stressed. "Past tense. I don't feel that way about him anymore." But something in the way she held herself as she said it made me think she wasn't being completely honest.

I decided not to push her for the time being. "What did he say when you told him you had feelings for him?"

She slapped her hands over her face, muffling the pained groan she released. "I don't want to say. It was so humiliating."

I reached up and took hold of her wrist, slowly pulling her hand down so she could see the sincerity in my eyes when I said, "You never have any reason to be embarrassed around me. I'm your friend. And I'd never judge you."

She gave me a tiny smile. "You really are an amazing friend. You know that?"

"The feeling is more than mutual, Len. And, hey, if you don't want to talk about it, you don't have to. I will respect whatever you decide."

"No, it's okay. I'll tell you. I need to tell *someone*. This has been eating me alive for months." She took a bracing breath. "When I told him I liked him, he basically said it was never going to happen. I was his friend's little sister, and was practically still a kid."

I sucked in a sharp breath. "He did *not* call you a kid."

She nodded. "He said I was too young to really know

what I wanted, and he was flattered, but he didn't see me that way."

"Of all the condescending, bullshit excuses . . . You know what? He *is* an asshole."

Lennix's eyes got wide, and she let out a bubble of surprised laughter. "Wow, babe. Aside from when you were stomping those roses to death, I don't think I've heard you curse that much."

I smiled bashfully. "I've tried to tone it down since I got Levi, but I think this moment called for it."

She lifted her glass. "Amen to that. Anyway, sure, I was crushed he didn't feel the same way I did, but I tried to get past it. It was awkward around him for a while, but I did my best to put it out of my mind and go back to normal. I thought we were finally moving beyond all the awkwardness when, all of a sudden, this switch flipped in him. Now it's like he goes out of his way to make me all rage-y. I've started fantasizing about all the different places on the ranch where I could hide his body so it would never be found."

"Well, if you ever need a hand with that, you can always call me. Tristan has a shovel, and I'm really good at keeping secrets."

She shot in my direction and wrapped her arms around me, yanking me into a hug so tight it made my ribs creak. For a tiny thing, she was strong as hell. "I'm so glad you came back to Hope Valley. I hate everything that asshole put you through while you were here, but I'm still glad, because it means I got a new friend for life."

The sting of tears came on the heels of her proclamation. I pulled back with a sniffle and gave her an accusatory glare. "If you make me cry right now I'm going to be so mad." She giggled, but didn't look the least bit apologetic. "But I feel the same way. You have no idea how much meeting you guys and becoming friends has helped me move past all the ugliness from before."

She sniffled and waved her hands in front of her face. "Now who's gonna make who cry?"

We talked for a while longer, the rest of the conversation much lighter, but after a while she had to get back to work. The lunch crowd had filtered off, and she needed to start preparing for the night crowd that would be much bigger and a lot rowdier.

I still had some time to kill before I had to pick Levi up from school, so I headed to the grocery store to grab something to make for dinner.

I'd lived in Hope Valley for more than seven years by the time I left Warren, but in all that time, I'd never gotten to know the people in town. Back then, I'd walked through the grocery store at a quick pace, keeping my head down and trying my hardest not to make eye contact with anyone. I was in and out, never long enough to make any type of connection. Seven years, and practically everyone I'd crossed paths with was a stranger.

Since coming back—since Tristan came into my life—so much had changed. As I steered the cart through the aisles of Fresh Foods, I had a smile on my face for every single person I passed. I recognized at least half of the people I saw, and more than once, I was stopped to make small talk.

For the first time since I moved here, I was actually a part of the town—of the community. For so long I'd been scared no one would believe me. Warren's charm and easy lies would fool them all.

Now I realized those worries had been planted in my head by Warren. The more time that passed, the more people were coming to me saying how sorry they were for what I'd gone through. The support of the community he'd once had was long gone now. The mask had been peeled away, and everyone was seeing him for what he was.

He was still doing everything in his power to drag this divorce out, but I wasn't worried. I was patient, and I knew the day would come when I'd finally be free of him. I was sure Tristan would come up with some elaborate way to celebrate, and I couldn't wait to see what he'd do.

I took my time shopping, planning out a dinner menu in my head that the guys in my life would enjoy enough they'd let the sight of vegetables on their plate slide.

They both seemed to be fans of my fried chicken, so I decided to make tenders with loaded mashed potatoes and green beans on the side.

I was not giving up my fight to make Levi like vegetables. One of two things was going to happen. Either he'd learn to love them, or I'd end up scarring him for life and he'd never eat another vegetable again. But I figured he'd be grown by then, and it wouldn't be my problem anymore.

To soften the blow, I picked up a chocolate cake from the bakery. It wasn't going to be as good as one of Nona's cakes, but it would work in a pinch.

I'd learned, growing up, Nona had done what her kids referred to as stress baking. According to the stories they shared over the family dinners Levi and I had been attending regularly, Tristan and Blythe would come home from school to find every surface of the kitchen covered in some sort of baked good. Legend had it she managed to supply an entire bake sale all by herself, and Tristan said he and his step-brother Shawn were the most popular kids on their soccer team because Nona always showed up at their games with trays of cupcakes.

Apparently the trait was genetic and had been passed town to Blythe, but it had manifested differently with her. She didn't stress bake, she stress cooked. Only, she'd taken that skill and made it into a career when she decided to open her own little catering company. It was still new, but she was excited about what her future held.

The more time I spent with Tristan's family, the more I loved them, and was excited to meet his step-sibling, and his and Blythe's half-brother, Liam, when they all traveled back home for Christmas.

It was the same for Levi. He'd already declared that Blythe's middle daughter, Adeline, was his best friend, with her other two, Avett and Ainsley, coming in at a close, collective second.

I checked out, taking a moment to chat with the cashier who I'd become friendly with over the past few months, and headed to my car. I was in the middle of loading everything into the back hatch when a shadow came up behind me, suddenly blocking out the sun. Before I had a chance to turn around, something cold and hard was pressed into my back.

"Scream, and I swear to God, I'll fucking shoot you."

My blood turned to ice at the sound of Warren's voice hissing in my ear.

"What—"

"Shut the fuck up," he clipped, jabbing the object

into my ribs hard enough to hurt. "Here's what you're going to do. You're going to leave your purse in the car and casually step away. Then you're going to get into the passenger seat of the one beside you. You aren't going to scream or try to run or do anything else to draw attention to yourself, understand?"

I struggled to swallow past the knot in my throat. Unable to form words, I nodded.

"Good girl. Now get moving."

I turned, glancing down to see that it had been the barrel of a gun he'd shoved into my ribs. My whole body began to tremble as terror dumped into my bloodstream. I scanned the parking lot, praying that someone would walk by as I slowly did what Warren had ordered. I knew the worst thing I could do was let him take me to a second location, but from the manic way he was watching me, there was no doubt in my mind he would pull that trigger if I gave him any reason.

With no other choice, I climbed into the passenger seat of the gray sedan that had parked beside my car and pulled the door closed.

Warren rounded the hood quickly and dropped into the driver's seat. Then, before I could ask him what the hell he planned on doing, his arm shot out and he slammed the butt of the gun into my temple. And everything went black.

Chapter Twenty-Eight

Tristan

My brain felt sluggish, like it was covered in cobwebs.

Since finding out from Merritt that Warren had known at least three of the victims, not to mention her brother, Harrison and I had started looking for any possible connections he could have had with the remaining ones. We'd gotten a warrant for his financial records, and for the past week, had been slogging through the mounds and mounds of documentation.

It had been slow and tedious, going through the man's bank records and personal life, and so far, we'd come up empty-handed.

While we hadn't found any leads on the case, I'd discovered his finances weren't as well off as he'd led Merritt to believe. In fact, he was on the brink of bankruptcy. His bank account was overdrawn, he was in considerable debt, and the more I dug, the more it looked like the charity work he did wasn't all exactly above board. He'd taken out a second mortgage on the house and wasn't paying it back.

Even his consulting company had been leveraged to the hilt, but from everything I'd gathered, I couldn't figure out where the money was ending up. None of it made any sense.

"Tris, I think I might have something," Harrison said, pulling my attention away from my computer screen. I'd stared at a spreadsheet and numbers for so long I felt like I was going blind.

Standing up, I moved to his side of the desk and braced my palms on top of it, looking down at the documents he'd been flipping through for the past four hours. "What do you have?"

He ran his pen along the highlighted line. "I've come across mention of this Advanced Aeronautics in Bell's records at least five times now, so I decided to trace it back and see what I could find. Apparently it's a company that designs and builds luxury aircrafts. Not for commercial use, but for the assholes who prefer to cruise around on private jets."

He riffled through the stacks of papers on his desk and unearthed the sheet he was hunting for, pulling it out and setting it on top of everything else. "Over the past year, several large deposits have been made into accounts for this company." He looked up at me, and I didn't miss the twinkle in his eye. "Curious as to who those checks came from?"

I pushed off his desk and stood to my full height, crossing my arms over my chest. "Let me guess . . . our remaining vics?"

He tapped the tip of his nose. "Bingo. Four of our ODs made substantial payments into those accounts, including Matthew Wright. The guy Merritt IDed as the guy she saw Bell arguing with at that banquet."

I looked at the list of names, my brows pulling together. "Okay, but what about Walter Reeves? I don't see his name here as an investor in Advanced Aeronautics."

"Ah, and you see, that's where things get interesting." Harrison rubbed his hands together gleefully. "I noticed that, despite the large deposits, the money never stayed in those accounts for long. I followed it and found it was being transferred into one single, off-shore account for a totally different shell corporation. "Guess who's listed as the owners of that shell corp?"

"Warren Bell."

"And Walter Reeves."

Letting out a gust of breath, I reached up and

dragged a hand through my hair. "Christ. He and Reeves were scamming their friends into investing in a bogus company, then stealing the money."

"My guess is he's also been killin' them off one by one when they came knockin', wanting to know where the hell their money went."

A picture started forming in my mind, and finally, everything became clearer. "Reeves was the first victim. I'm willing to bet Warren got greedy and didn't want to split everything they'd stolen."

Harrison rocked back in his chair, twirling a pen between his fingers. "That's not a bet I'd take, since I'm pretty sure you're right."

This asshole really was a piece of work. There wasn't a single honest thing about him. His entire life had been carefully curated to make him out to be something other than what he was. He wasn't a successful businessman. His own company was barely staying afloat. He wasn't a man of means, and he certainly wasn't a great philanthropist. On top of being an abusive piece of shit, he was also a crook and a thief.

I smiled as everything finally came together. "It's only speculation at this point, but I'm sure it's enough to get a judge to sign a warrant that'll basically let us turn his life upside down."

Harrison folded his arms behind his head and kicked his feet onto his desk. "Only one way to find out."

"You get started on that paperwork and I'll fill Cap in on what we found." I huffed out a breath. "Goddamn, it feels good to have finally figured this one out." And it was an added bonus that it led back to Warren Bell in a way that would probably lead to some serious jail time.

I was about to head up to Hayes office when a collective groan moved through the bullpen. I didn't have to look to know who'd just walked in—without permission, once again.

With a resigned sigh, I turned to face Sue Ellen Mayfield as she stomped her way over to me.

"You've got to be fuckin' kidding?" Hayes grunted under his breath. "Does she really not have anything better to do?"

"Apparently not," I answered right before she closed in. "Ms. Mayfield," I started, not bothering with a smile or a polite greeting this time. "Now, ma'am, you know you're not allowed back here without permission."

"I wouldn't have to bust my way in here if you people would do your damn jobs. I've called three times to complain that my neighbor has planted an azalea bush that crosses the property line into my yard by five inches. Three times, and no one has come out to do a damn thing. You've left me no choice but to come here in person." She stomped her foot and crossed her arms, her hip cocked out as she glared daggers my way. "I am done being blown off. I want to know what you're going to do about this."

The answer was nothing. We—or me, specifically—weren't going to do anything about a bush five inches over an invisible line.

"Ms. Mayfield, if the bush is that big of a nuisance, why don't you trim back what's on your side?"

Her chin jerked back as she huffed in affront. "So now it's my job to handle it when my neighbor breaks the law?"

A headache was forming behind my eyeballs. I couldn't take it any longer. I'd officially reached my limit where this woman was concerned. "There are no laws being broken. You're a bitter, miserable woman who spends her day searching for anything under the sun to be angry about. And when you can't find anything, you invent it! Your neighbors haven't done a damn thing to you other than exist, but apparently, even that is offensive to you somehow. If anyone has cause for complaint, it's the people on your block, because they're stuck having to live next to you!"

"Oh shit," Harrison muttered as soon as I finished my diatribe.

Sue Ellen's jaw dropped as she rocked back on her

heel. "How dare you speak to me like that? I have half a mind to go straight to the mayor and file a complaint against you for—"

"Then do it! Christ, please, stop threatening and do it already. At least then you'll be raining your special brand of misery on town hall instead of here."

"What in the hell is goin' on down here?" Hayes called out as he stormed into the bullpen.

"What's going on is that I'm being verbally assaulted by one of your detectives," Sue Ellen accused.

I was about to point out that it was her company that was the assault when my cell started ringing.

I twisted away from Hayes and Sue Ellen, who were now trading barbs in front of the entire department, and pulled the phone from my pocket. I swiped the screen without looking to see who was calling and brought it to my ear. "Fanning," I answered.

"Mr. Fanning?" a voice I didn't recognized asked.

"Yes."

"This is Judith from Hope Valley Elementary. We're calling to see if you would be picking Levi up this afternoon. We have him in our office right now."

I glanced at my watch and saw that school had gotten out thirty minutes ago. "His aunt is supposed to have picked him up already," I said as a chill moved down my spine.

"Yes, that was what I thought. But we've tried calling Ms. Bell a few times and can't get through."

My muscles locked up tight and everything around me faded away. "She didn't answer?"

"No, sir. And it's unusual for her to be late."

It was more than unusual. It just plain wouldn't happen if Merritt could control it. Levi was her number one priority, and there was no way in hell she would ever be late to pick him up. Unless something was wrong. "Thank you for calling. Someone will be there to get him soon."

I disconnected the call and scrolled through my phone to Merritt's number. My heart began racing as it rang and rang in my ear before voicemail kicked in.

"Goddamn it," I growled, hanging up and trying again. "Come on, baby, pick up," I pleaded under my breath. "Pick up. Please." I got voicemail for the second time.

Reading the energy coming off me, Hayes walked over and placed his hand on my shoulder. "What's goin' on?"

"Merritt didn't show up to get Levi." I looked at him as my heart fell out of my chest, saying the words I never wanted to say. "I think something bad has happened."

Chapter Twenty-Nine

Merritt

I rolled over with a groan, my skull pounding like it had been cracked in two. I blinked my eyes open and the sunlight coming in the widow felt like an ice pick in my brain.

I tried again, more carefully this time. When I was finally able to open them enough to take in my surroundings, nothing was familiar about the room I was in. My memory was hazy, and I felt like I had the world's worst hangover, but that couldn't have been the case. I didn't remember drinking anything.

I thought back, trying to recall what had happened leading up to me waking up in this room. I remember going to see Lennix and the conversation we had about Raylan. I remember going to the grocery store afterward to pick up something for dinner before I had to get Levi.

Levi.

I shot up as my nephew's name filled my head. My stomach revolted at the movement and my head grew woozy; I thought for a second I was going to be sick. I breathed deeply, in through my nose and out through my mouth, until the nausea abated. But the panic was still there. I was supposed to pick him up from school. But I hadn't made it. Why hadn't I—Oh god. Oh God no.

Memories came barreling back, whipping through my head like they were on fast forward, and with them, a racing heart and fear-induced tears.

The parking lot of Fresh Foods. Warren. The gun.

I remembered getting in his car, then it all just . . . stopped. He had to have knocked me out. Lifting a hand, I gingerly prodded at my left temple. There was a huge knot on the side of my head—the source of the headache and dizziness, no doubt, and when I pulled my fingers back, I saw blood.

His gun. I remembered he'd hit me in the side of the head with the butt of his gun.

My gaze darted around the space again as I tried my hardest to figure out where the hell I was. The room contained a single square table with two chairs and a twin-sized cot I was currently sitting on. That was it as far as furniture went. There was a tiny galley kitchenette in the back right corner with two countertops, a single row of three cabinets, a hot plate, a toaster oven, and a mini-fridge. There was an old cast iron wood-burning fireplace in the back left corner, and a single window with iron bars. The space was completely utilitarian, and from the dust and cobwebs everywhere, it looked like no one had been in it for several years.

I carefully stood, holding my arms out for balance as the world tilted. I knew for certain I had a concussion, and it was a bad one. But I couldn't let it keep me from trying to figure out where I was, and more importantly, how to get the hell out.

I checked the window and saw that it had been painted shut at some point. Not that it mattered since there was no way I was getting through those bars. I tiptoed across the room and gripped the doorknob, holding my breath as I slowly tried giving it a turn, but it didn't budge. It had been a long shot, hoping Warren hadn't locked me in, but the disappointment still burned in my gut as I struggled to keep the panic attack at bay.

I had to figure this out.

The good news was he hadn't tied me up. I knew how he thought, and I knew he hadn't bothered because he assumed I was still the same weak, scared, obedient wife. His arrogance wouldn't let him consider anything else. And I could use that to my advantage. I just had to figure out how.

I checked the kitchenette next, opening the cabinets quietly. There was a dusty plate covered in rat droppings and a glass with a dead bug in the bottom of it, but that was it. I grew disheartened as I moved to the two drawers. They were my last hope. The first one was empty, but in the second, there was an old, rusty Swiss Army knife. The blade had been broken off, but the cork screw was still attached. It would have to do.

I quickly popped out the curling piece of metal so it was ready to go when time came to use it, and stuffed it into my pocket.

Footsteps sounded somewhere outside the door, and I quickly raced back to the cot, ignoring the throb in my skull and my churning stomach. I sat down as the lock clicked and the door opened.

Warren stood in the frame. "Oh good. You're awake." He smiled in a way that sent a chill up my neck and made the little hairs on my arms stand on end. "Punishing you while you're unconscious wouldn't have been any fun."

TRISTAN

. . .

I PACED the stretch of asphalt behind Merritt's car, raking my hands through my hair. It hadn't taken long for a call to come in about an abandoned SUV in the parking lot of Fresh Foods. Harrison and I had raced out of the station, Hayes closely on our heels. When we got there, I spotted the vehicle immediately. The back hatch was opened, two plastic grocery bags sitting on the black carpeting, along with her purse. But the cart was still there with Merritt's remaining bags inside. It was like she'd vanished into thin air in the middle of unloading her groceries.

There was no sign of her anywhere. No blood, no evidence of a struggle. And no one had seen a thing. She was just . . . gone. Her keys, phone, and wallet were with her purse, so I couldn't track her location.

The only thing holding me together was my skin. Blythe had rushed to the school to get Levi, and she was keeping him entertained. I'd asked her not to tell him Merritt was missing yet. If the time came when he had to know, I wanted to be the one to tell him, and I wanted to be there in case he crumpled.

I'd put in calls to everyone I knew. The Hope Valley grapevine had been activated, and there were currently people searching all across town. Rhodes had split his guys into teams, some searching digitally, some with boots on the ground.

So far no one had turned up anything. I couldn't accept that we might not find her. Couldn't accept the thought of a life without her. Not when I just got her.

Patrol cars filled the lot. Police were canvassing, but every minute that passed where I didn't hear from her felt like an eternity in hell.

"We'll find her," Hayes assured me, coming up and clapping me on the shoulder. "We've got the whole town lookin', son. We'll find her."

Harrison came running up holding a tablet in his hand. "Got it!" he shouted as he ducked under the police tape that had been stretched out and rushed up to us. "I got the security footage."

"Show me."

He used his finger to rewind the digital image, then tapped play. No one said a word or breathed too loud as we watched Merritt open the back of her car and start loading bags in. She was totally unaware of the person climbing out of the car beside her until it was too late.

The figure in a dark hoodie moved in behind her, and my entire body stiffened at the same time Merritt's image did. The two of them stayed like that for a few seconds before the man took two steps away, but it was enough space for the camera to catch the gun he had in his hand.

"Goddamn it," I hissed as the scene continued to

play out. There was no audio, so I didn't know for certain what he'd said to get her into his car, but I could imagine. As soon as Merritt was in the passenger seat, the man rounded the hood of the car, scanning the parking lot as he went, providing the perfect angle to see his face.

"Fuckin' knew it!" I growled. I'd known all along it was him, and now there was poof. I was going to make him pay.

My cell started buzzing in my back pocket, and I pulled it out to see Rhodes's name flashing across the screen. It wasn't too long ago he'd been in my shoes when Blythe had been taken, so if there was anyone I trusted to help me get my girl back, it was him.

"Just got video confirmation it was Bell. Tell me you got somethin'."

I'd gone with my gut, and as Harrison drove us from the station to the grocery store earlier, I'd put in a call to Rhodes, telling him to dig up everything he could find on her ex, and to start with property records. He was spiraling, but he wasn't stupid enough to take her back to his house. So he had to have another place in mind.

"There wasn't anything in his name other than the house we already knew about. But I searched that shell corp like you asked, and I got a hit."

"Where?"

"He bought the abandoned lumber mill up on Tolliver Mill Road. Place has been abandoned for years. It would be the perfect place to go."

My feet started moving before he finished talking. "Heading that way now."

"Meet you there, brother. And Tris, I know what this is doin' to you right now. Keep it together, brother. We're gonna get your girl back."

MERRITT

EVERYTHING HURT. Every cell. Every nerve. I'd witnessed Warren's cruelty more times than I could count, but it had never been like this.

Each strike left behind its mark, and he'd hit and kicked me so many times I'd lost track of all my injuries. He'd split the skin at my cheekbone and my right eye was quickly swelling shut. My nose was bleeding, and I'd chipped a tooth. But other than my ribs, I didn't think he'd broken anything.

At least not yet.

I fought to remain conscious, knowing I needed to be

able to move when I saw my opening, but it was getting hard with every punch and kick.

He'd raged and screamed and cursed me as he inflicted his punishment.

"This is all your fucking fault!" he seethed as his fist slammed into my stomach, knocking the breath from my lungs. If you hadn't spread your whore legs for that backwoods hick cop, he wouldn't be investigating me!"

I didn't know what he was talking about, but I couldn't afford to focus any of my energy on that. Not when I needed every ounce of it to keep from passing out.

He yanked my hair back and got in my face, his lips curled back from his teeth as he seethed, "Did you have fun? Huh? Did you enjoy bein' a whore for him? Did it feel good to act like a slut? Fuckin' another man while you were married?"

I grunted as he tossed me to the floor, that goddamn loafer pulling back and slamming into my hip.

"To think, I wasted all that time on a dirty little slut like you. Should've known you were never worth it." He bent down and grabbed my arm, yanking me back to my feet. I cried out as my bones and muscles protested. My entire body felt like one big, throbbing bruise, and I wasn't sure how much more I could take. "Waste of my fuckin' time, playing your brother the way I did. His ass should've died just like the rest of them, but that stupid little brat had to call for help and saved him."

He must have seen the way my one good eye flared in shock, because he grinned evilly. "That's right. It was me; I knew the only way you'd ever come back was if that fuckin' kid needed you. Took almost no effort at all. Just showed up at your brother's door and showed him what I had; he was all too eager to stick that needle in his arm."

It was all his fault, I thought as burning tears fell from my good eye, the salt burning the cuts on my face.

Fisting the front of my shirt, Warren yanked me onto my toes, forcing my face closer to his. "Maybe I should do myself a favor and end you too. Rid myself of your pathetic, whiny, broken ass. I'll put the needle in your arm myself. Do the world a favor. What do you say?"

This was it. This was the closest I was ever going to get. My opening was right in front of me, so I took it. Reaching into my pocket, I yanked out the cork screw and stabbed it right into his neck where it met his shoulder.

Warren let out a roar of pain as I ripped the twisted metal out and stabbed it back in again until he lost his hold on my shirt.

He bellowed in pain, releasing me to reach up and cup the gaping wound I'd created. It was a miracle I didn't collapse when he released me. I didn't know what kind of damaged I'd done, if I hit an artery or what, but I didn't have time to stick around and find out.

I took off running as Warren's other-worldly bellows echoed all around me. His footsteps were like shotgun blasts as he ran after me, screaming my name in a voice that would give me nightmares for a good, long while.

I heard him getting closer, but I couldn't stop. I still didn't know where I was. I didn't have the first clue where I was going, but I knew I couldn't let him get me again. I skidded around a corner, my feet slipping from under me, but I managed to stay upright and put on a burst of speed that was fed by pure adrenaline and the will to live.

I made Tristan a promise that if anything ever happened, and he wasn't there to protect me, I would fight with everything I had. And that was exactly what I was doing.

I raced down a long hall and cut a sharp right when I reached the end. The sound of his gun going off made me jump as fragments of the wall near my head blew outward and scratched at my face. He'd just shot at me, the bullet missing by only inches.

I pushed myself impossibly faster, lifting my arms to shield my head when he fired again, the bullet lodging into the wall about two feet in front of me.

Each inhale felt like I was breathing fire into my lungs. I could barely see where I was going. But I didn't stop. I cleared a large, open space, and nearly cried out in relief when I spotted a door.

Warren's steps thundered after me, that demonic voice even closer now, still screaming my name as I reached for the knob.

What happened next seemed to happen in slow motion. My hand grasped the knob and turned. I yanked the door open and let my momentum carry me through, not realizing there would be people on the other side. Tristan's face was the first one I saw. As soon as I crossed the threshold, he banded his arms around my waist, whipping me up and around right as another gunshot went off. I'd been moving so fast that my body didn't stop when it collided with his. We both went down to the ground, Tristan on top of me, putting himself between me and the monster I'd been running from. A moment later, there were more. So many it sounded like there were multiple guns being fired.

I slapped my hands over my ears, slammed my eyes closed, and screamed until the noise around me stopped.

It could have been an eternity or only a handful of seconds, but when I felt Tristan's fingers skate over my jaw, I opened my eyes and the first thing I saw was that beautiful sky blue.

Chapter Thirty

Merritt

Two months later

I PULLED the fruit tray out of the fridge and placed it on the island, pulling off the top and removing the lid from the container of dip in the middle.

Taking a step back, I surveyed everything. I had to make sure I didn't miss a thing, I'd gotten everything right, down to the very last detail. This day had to be perfect.

Tristan moved into the kitchen just as I began reorganizing all the platters and trays taking up the island and counter top.

"Dandelion, it all looks great. Stop stressing." He came up behind me and grabbed my hips, leaning in to press a kiss to the side of my neck.

I looked back at him over my shoulder. "Great's not perfect, Tristan. I need this to be *perfect*."

"It's a birthday party for an eight-year-old," he reminded me. "You're putting too much pressure on yourself."

Okay, yes. It was Levi's birthday party, but given what Levi had gone through during his eighth year of life, I wanted to make sure this day went off without a hitch. He deserved nothing less.

After Warren had taken me, there was a spell where things became pretty rocky. There was no way to hide my battered body from him, and the first time Levi walked into my hospital room after the ordeal was finally over, he'd burst into tears. He'd been so scared of hurting me more that he'd refused to touch me for three whole days. And those days would go down in history as some of the worst of my life for that very reason.

Seeing his aunt like that had caused him to backslide a bit, and he started having nightmares where he lost me forever.

I hadn't hesitated to find the best therapist in the area for kids his age, and within a week of that first nightmare, he'd had his first appointment. The road to healing wasn't fast or straight, but he was getting back to where he'd been before Warren had abducted and tortured me.

Speaking of healing, the events of that day had left a mark on me as well, and I didn't mean only physically. The fear I felt at never seeing Levi and Tristan again had refused to let me go for a long time. It helped I knew I would never have to fear Warren again. What I hadn't been able to see as everything was happening was that Tristan hadn't been standing outside that door by himself. They'd already been on their way to rescue me when I stabbed Warren and made a run for it. They'd heard the gunshots and Warren's scream, so they knew which building around the abandoned mill I'd been trapped in. Turned out, it was an old dormitory for the people who worked nights, and that's where he'd been keeping me.

As soon as Tristan got me clear and Warren had taken that first shot, Rhodes and Tristan's partner, Harrison, had fired back, killing him instantly.

I found out later he would have died no matter what. I'd managed to nick his artery, and he'd been slowly bleeding out already. I didn't know how to feel about the fact that I'd technically killed him before he was shot, and that, on top of seeing him lying on the ground dead, messed with my head in major ways.

Because of the post-traumatic stress both Tristan and

I had suffered, we decided the smart thing would be for us to seek professional help as well. It was working wonders to get us back to our light, beautiful life we'd had before.

"Dandelion, stop that and look at me," Tristan insisted gently, pulling my hands away when I started messing with the flower arrangement—because that was what every eight-year-old boy wanted for his birthday. A freaking flower arrangement. But I blamed it on not being in my right mind when I was putting all of this together.

I lifted my gaze to those blue eyes that saved me over and over again every time I looked into them, and a sense of calm washed over me. "You don't need to wear yourself out like this. He's going to love it." He looked around the house, raising his brows and said, "It looks like the *WWE* threw up all over the place."

He had a point. I might have gone a little overboard with the decorations. But that was nothing compared to what I'd done outside. There was a wrestling themed bounce house, cotton candy, snow cone and popcorn machines, and under a large tent at the back of the yard were different stations where the kids could either get their faces painted, have a balloon animal made, or sit for a caricature portrait.

"I know. And I promise I'll tone it down next year, but Ozzy never did anything for any of Levi's birthdays."

Tristan's face fell and he let out a low growl. "You know, the more you tell me about him, the gladder I am that the stupid prick got his sentence extended."

I was glad for that too, and I didn't care if that made me a bad sister. Apparently Ozzy caused as much trouble *inside* prison as he had outside of it. When he started a fight in the prison yard and ended up stabbing somebody, a sentence that had only been eighteen months had five years added to it.

That was all the judge needed to hear to strip his parental rights away and grant me full and permanent custody.

Hearing that had gone a long way in healing Levi.

Warren was gone and Ozzy was out of our lives forever. And I wanted today to reflect all that good. In my head, this was our first step into the future as a family.

The front door opened, and Nona's voice called out, "We're here."

"In the kitchen," I returned. Smiling brightly as she and Trick rounded the corner with Doc on their heels.

"I have the cake," Nona told me, sliding the large bakery box she'd been holding onto the counter. "And I have to say, this might be my best one yet."

"Not that we'd know for sure since she wouldn't let anyone taste it," Trick grumbled as he dropped a huge present wrapped in wrestling-themed wrapping paper on the dining room table with all the other presents. I didn't know what they got him, but I knew it was going to be good. They'd really taken to spoiling him over the past few months, treating Levi the exact same as they did Blythe's kids. It was as if Nona and Trick had decided to step into the role of grandparents, while Blythe and Rhodes were a sort of surrogate aunt and uncle.

Tristan's mom shot him a dull look. "First taste goes to the birthday boy. You know that." Her eyes darted around the room as I lifted the lid to the cake box and took a peek. She was right. It was perfection.

"Speaking of the birthday boy, where is he?" Nona asked, her excitement to see Levi clear as day.

"Blythe and Rhodes took him and the kids for a birthday breakfast and to ride go-carts so we'd have time to set up everything before guests arrive."

I'd taken invitations to the school and given them to his teacher, asking that she give one to every classmate. I hadn't expected they'd all come, of course. But when the RSVPs started rolling in, it became clear that Levi really was as popular as he claimed.

At least fifteen kids and their parents stuffed into our backyard then, along with the rest of our friends and loved ones, all waiting to surprise the boy of the hour.

It was on that thought that the front door opened again, and what sounded like a herd of elephants came racing through.

Levi skidded to a stop, his eyes bulging and mouth hanging open. "*Wow!*" he practically shouted. "This is the coolest thing *ever!*"

"Happy Birthday, buddy," I said, reaching out to pull him into a hug. He told me a few weeks ago he'd officially outgrown me picking him up, and I was very proud of myself for making it until he left for school before breaking down in ugly, sobbing tears.

"This is all for me?"

Tristan ruffled his hair. "Sure is, kiddo. A boy only turns eight once, and that day has to be celebrated." A smile curled my lips up. "Why don't you go out back and see what else we've done."

He raced for the back door, the rest of us following closely behind. The instant he blasted through, everyone shouted, "*Happy Birthday!*"

My little guy froze, his eyes scanning over everyone crowded around the yard. As his eyes tracked over every person, his little chin began to tremble and his eyes filled with tears.

Tristan and I crouched down in front of him.

"Honey, what's wrong?" I asked quietly, reaching out to brush back the flop of hair that was always falling into his eyes. At the contact, he lunged, wrapping his arms around my neck and squeezing.

"I've never had a birthday party before," he rasped against my skin. Before his words had a chance to penetrate, he released me and lunged for Tristan, giving him the same treatment, and I heard his emotion-clogged voice croak, "This is the best day of my life."

It only took another second for him to regain his composure, but once he did, he practically forgot all about us as he charged toward his friends.

I sniffled, doing my best not to cry as Tristan pulled me into his side. Together, we watched as Levi was showered with more love.

"I can't believe he's already eight," I lamented. I didn't want to feel sad on such a joyous day, but it was hard not to think about how fast my little guy was growing up. "I'm not ready for him to get older."

Tristan leaned down and pressed a kiss to my temple. "You know, if you wanted, we could always start from scratch."

My eyes shot up to his. "Are you saying you want to have kids?"

"With you, Dandelion, I want to have everything."

Epilogue

Tristan

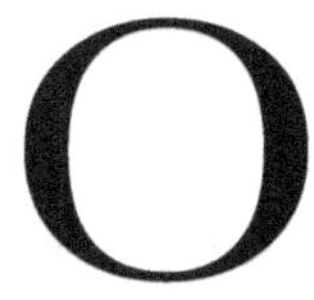*ne month later*

"Is the blindfold really necessary?" Merritt asked from the passenger seat for the fifth time in less than fifteen minutes.

"For the fifth time, yes," I answered, humor laced through my words as I pulled my Suburban into the parking spot and shifted into park.

"Aunt Merri, you're gonna be *so* surprised," Levi said on a giddy little laugh.

I turned to the back seat and shot him a wink. He

attempted to return it, but ended up blinking both of his eyes.

"You ready, buddy?"

He nodded earnestly and unbuckled his seatbelt. "Yup."

"All right then. Let's do this."

With Levi's help, I got Merritt out of the car and into the warehouse, and in true Merritt fashion, she'd grumbled about the blindfold the entire way. Once she was in place and I flipped on the lights, he started hopping from foot to foot, his excitement practically bursting right out of him.

"Now, Tris? Can I say it?"

I let out a chuckle and nodded. "Yeah, little man. You can say it."

He threw his arms out and shouted, "*Surprise,*" just as I whipped Merritt's blindfold off. She squinted against the lights and blinked her eyes into focus, and as soon as she realized what she was looking at, her lips parted on an O and her eyes filled with tears.

All of the pieces she'd been working on had been moved from the garage to here, with plenty of room for more. All of her tools and supplies were organized neatly along the shelves. It had taken a while to get everything set up, but with help from Levi and my friends, we got it done. "You got me a workshop?"

"You were running out of space in the garage, and I wanted you to be able to keep doing what you love."

A tear slipped free and trailed down her cheek as she whispered, "You got me a warehouse." Then she threw herself into my arms.

I rocked back on my foot with a laugh. "I take it that means you like it?"

She pulled back and cupped my cheeks, her sage green eyes dancing with happiness. "No, Tristan. I love it. And I love you." She lifted up on her toes to kiss me, but Levi busted in before that could happen.

"There's more! No kissing 'til the end. Even though kissing is super gross."

Merritt giggled as she looked between us. "There's more?"

I pulled her arms from around my neck and stepped back, slowly lowering down to one knee as I pulled the antique ring from my pocket and held it up.

She slapped her hands over her mouth on a sharp gasp as those tears started coming faster and faster.

"Merritt, I never really gave much thought to what my future looked like until you came into my life and showed me how bright and wonderful it could be. With you, I know exactly what my forever is supposed to look like. I know it's worth chasing down and fighting for. So I'm asking you, will you give me that forever I've been chasing since the first moment I saw you?"

"Yes!" she shouted happily.

I shot to my feet and grabbed her hand, my own shaking as I slid the ring into place. Lifting her off her feet, I sealed my lips with hers and whipped her in a circle.

"Does this mean you guys are gonna start havin' babies??" Levi asked once we'd broken apart.

Looking at the boy who held the other half of my heart, I smiled so wide my cheeks ached. "Would it be okay with you if we did?"

The thoughtful look overtook his face as he tapped his chin. "Well, I've been thinkin' about it, and I decided it would be really cool to be a big brother."

And just when I thought my life couldn't possibly get any better, the two of them went and gave me more.

The End.

Thank you so much for reading!
Be on the lookout for book 5
Coming soon

Sneak Peek of The Best of Me

Want to know where Blythe got her start? Check out Nona and Trick's story, **THE BEST OF ME** now.

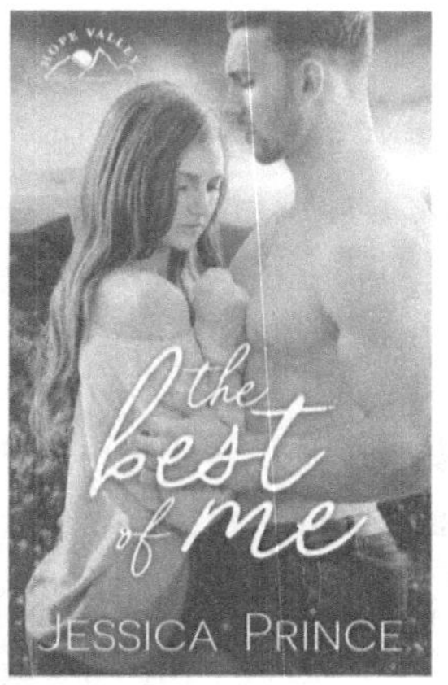

Prologue

Nona

There were three things in life that I knew as absolute fact.

First, a good blowout and pretty undergarments could work wonders in boosting a woman's confidence.

Second, the shitty, worthless men outnumbered the good by about ten to two.

And finally, Emma Wanderly was a raging idiot.

That last one might have seemed harsh, but it was the stone-cold truth. After all, she didn't just have a *good* man. She had one of the very best.

And that idiot went and threw him away.

Seeing as I spent years upon years married to the scummiest, lowest form of man there was, I considered myself somewhat of an expert in the field of men, especially when it came to telling the good from the bad. So I knew to my bones that my take on Patrick "Trick" Wanderly was spot-on.

I'd see him and his family around town and wish I were lucky enough to have a man like that in my life. A man who didn't shy away from showing affection to his wife in public, letting her and everyone else around know just how much he loved her with nothing but a touch or caress or simply a look. A man who'd watch his kids and smile or shake his head good-naturedly, like he got a kick out of them acting like typical rowdy children. He was a man content with all the blessings in his life and wasn't afraid to show it.

Don't get me wrong, my kids were absolutely everything to me, and each morning when they woke up and came stumbling into the kitchen, groggy and cranky with sleep, I knew just how lucky I was.

But in all our years of marriage, Christian had never looked at me or touched me the way Trick looked at and touched Emma. In public or in private. And for that reason, I couldn't help the twinge of jealousy that shot through my heart every time I saw them together.

Then, almost out of the blue, the picture-perfect couple was no more. I was baffled. Hell, all of Hope Valley was in a tizzy, struggling to figure out what had happened.

One second they seemed to have it all, and the next... *poof*. It was gone.

I didn't get it. Trick was sweet and incredibly kind. He was thoughtful, always putting others first. He was so funny I spent most of the time in his presence laughing until my stomach ached. And if all of that hadn't been enough, he was, hands down, the sexiest, most handsome man I'd ever laid eyes on.

Sandy brown hair clipped short in an easy-tomanage yet attractive style put his gorgeous features on display. A strong, square jaw that was always covered in a day's worth of light brown stubble, a straight, masculine nose, and eyes the most stunning gunmetal gray were only the tip of the iceberg that made Trick Wanderly all that he was. Broad shoulders led to a wide chest that eventually dipped into a trim waist. His strong arms were made to wrap around you and protect you from everything bad, and I'd fantasized about being in those arms more than was probably healthy.

It was those fantasies that made me turn around in the middle of a conversation I was having with friends and scan the massive crowd until my eyes finally found him. And the moment they did, my heart clenched so painfully it nearly stole my breath.

He looked miserable, heartbroken. *Devastated.* Like his whole world had been ripped out from beneath him.

I'd noticed that exact look on his face more times than I cared to count over the past months. A look he got whenever he thought no one would notice, or when he had too much on his mind and accidentally allowed that carefree mask to slip.

And every time I saw it, it broke my heart a little more.

I'd have given anything to be able to take that pain

away from him, to heal those wounds. But I knew firsthand that it wasn't that easy. The best I could do was be there for him, offering a shoulder to lean on, an ear to listen, or a stiff drink when talking just wasn't going to cut it.

Offering my friends a distracted "I need a refill, be back," I found myself moving around the elegantly adorned tables beneath the canvas and twinkle lights of the romantic tent like I had tunnel vision.

I was halfway across the tent where Hayes and my girl Tempie were holding their wedding reception when Trick's head came up. It was almost as if he sensed me moving in his direction. Those beautiful gray eyes locked with mine and that sadness melted away, replaced with a smile that made my knees weak and my belly quiver.

My lips tipped up of their own accord, offering him a small grin in return, and the sway of my hips grew a little more pronounced as I closed the rest of the distance.

"Officer," I greeted teasingly.

The low, rich chuckle that rolled from his chest felt like a gift. "Darlin'," he returned. "You havin' a good time?"

"I am. Good food, good people, celebration. Makes for a great night."

That shadow slid over his face once more before he tamped it down. "I hear that."

"How about you?"

He knocked back the last of the amber liquid in his glass and raised a finger to the bartender for another. As soon as his fresh drink was placed in front of him, he lifted it and slugged back half in one gulp, telling me what frame of mind he was in before he turned back to me with a smile that didn't even come close to meeting his eyes. "Yeah, sweetheart. I'm happy for them."

"Didn't ask if you were happy for them, honey," I murmured, leaning in close. "I asked if you were having a good time."

"Nona—" Just then, the band shifted from a fast tempo, peppy song to something slower and softer.

Curling my fingers around his big hand, I gave it a tug and commanded, "Come on, Officer. I'll let you take me for a spin on the floor."

He allowed me to pull him off his stool and lead him toward the makeshift dance floor, rolling his eyes playfully when I spun around and placed my free hand on his shoulder.

The small flutters I'd been feeling in my belly since his fingers closed around mine erupted the moment his large palm slid along my waist and settled on the small of my back. With Trick leading, we fell into an easy rhythm and moved in silence until I found the courage to say what I'd wanted to say since first approaching him.

"It gets easier," I murmured quietly. His eyes flashed to me, and I watched in panic as that beautiful gray grew intense and stormy. But the words were already out there, and there was no pulling them back.

In for a penny, in for a pound, Nona, I thought as I pulled in a steady breath.

"I won't tell you it gets better, but it does get easier. I promise, Trick."

Those clouds parted. His face went soft and sympathetic as he whispered, "Speaking from experience, darlin'?"

"You know I am," I replied sadly. There'd been no hiding it. The whole town knew about my failed marriage, and I was sure there were still rumblings going around about how stupid I'd been not to end it much sooner than I had. But I'd been in love, and when you loved someone so strongly that you built a life and a family together, throwing in the towel just wasn't that simple.

I'd made myself a promise when things started to turn from bad to worse. I was going to do whatever I could. I was going to fight and scratch and claw so *I knew* beyond the shadow of a doubt that I'd done everything in my power to make my marriage work. So when it was all said and done, I could hold my head up high, I could look at my kids and know I hadn't just given up when things got too hard.

Now it was over, and I spent every day with my head held high in the knowledge that I'd given it my all.

"Fuckin' idiot."

My chin jerked back and my eyes went wide at the venom in his voice. "Wh-what?"

"Christian Fanning," he answered, speaking my ex-husband's name in a rough, craggy growl. "Fuckin' idiot."

My head cocked to the side, and I felt my face go gentle as I looked up at him. "She's gonna hate herself," I whispered, and at my words, he closed his eyes as pain filtered across his handsome face.

"Nona—"

"She'll wake up one day and realize exactly what she lost. She'll realize she had it all and she just let it go, and she'll hate herself for it."

"Sweetheart—"

"You're an incredible man, Trick. Best man I've ever met."

The hand holding mine let go and came up, the pads of his fingers dragging gently along my cheekbone as he tucked my hair behind my ear. "That can't be true."

"It is," I declared forcefully. "Trust me, Trick. It's

true. I know shitty men. I know lazy men. I know all about worthless pieces of shit who don't care about anything or anyone but themselves. And *you aren't that*. You're amazing. And smart. And funny. And sexy —" My diatribe came to a screeching halt. I hadn't meant to say that last part out loud. Slamming my eyes closed, I hung my head in mortification as my cheeks caught fire.

He put pressure beneath my chin, forcing my head back up so he could see me. "Nona, darlin'."

I gave my head a shake. "Excuse me while I wait for the floor to open up and swallow me."

His body shook against mine, and I knew he was laughing, but I didn't find anything about this the slightest bit funny. "Come on, Nona. Open those pretty eyes for me." After a few more humiliating seconds, I peeled my eyelids open and nearly melted into a puddle at the warmth radiating from his gaze. "Means the world to me, honey, everything you just said. The absolute world."

"It's just... what I meant to say is I'm here, you know, if you ever need to talk. I get it... so I'm here. For you."

"You're pretty incredible yourself."

I lowered my eyes again as a fierce blush stole up my neck. "Thanks," I whispered shyly.

"And beautiful."

My head shot back up, my lips parting on a surprised inhale. "Th-thank you."

Something in his expression changed. It was as if he could suddenly read every thought in my head. The longing, the desire I'd felt for him for months. In an instant there was a flare of heat that hadn't been there just a moment before, so hot it turned the gray to liquid. The intensity of it made my knees buckle, and I would have hit the floor, embarrassing myself even further if it hadn't been for Trick's other arm banding around my waist and pulling me tight against him.

The look in his eyes was enough to make my breathing ragged as my heart pounded against my ribs.

"Trick," I panted as my breasts swelled and my nipples hardened.

"You wanna get outta here, sweetheart?"

I did. I *really* did. So I gave him a little nod and followed eagerly as he took my hand once more and led me from the dance floor and out of the tent, excitement coursing through my veins as I skipped to keep up.

A loud thump followed by a quietly hissed "Shit" startled me out of a dead sleep. I blinked my eyes as they slowly adjusted to the darkness surrounding me. My fuzzy brain had trouble recalling what was going on, but when I rolled toward the noise that had woken me, the twinge between my thighs was enough to bring the whole night back to me.

Trick dragging me from the wedding reception, loading me in his truck, and driving like a bat out of hell. The way his jagged voice abraded against my skin when he asked, "Your kids home?" and the soft breathiness of mine as I replied, "They're with their dad this weekend."

Everything that came after was completely and utterly out of this world. It was a dream come true. No, actually it was *better* than anything I could have dreamed up. *He* was better.

Trick Wanderly was the best lover I'd ever had—not that I had many to compare him to, but still. He'd fucked me hard and rough, he made love to me slow and gentle, he made me feel a million things I'd never felt before, and he spent hours doing it *thoroughly* until we both passed out from exhaustion.

My body ached in the most delectable ways from the workout he'd given it, and as I finished my roll, a smile spread across my face so wide my cheeks ached. That was, until I caught a glimpse of Trick's shadowed frame in the dark.

Twisting around quickly, I flicked on the lamp

beside my bed and spun back to him. "What are you doing?"

He finished pulling up the tuxedo slacks he'd been wearing before I slowly stripped him out of them hours earlier. His shirt was already on but unbuttoned, revealing tanned skin over ripped muscles from his chest all the way down to where that sexy V dipped into his waistband and the small smattering of hair sprinkled over his pecs. I'd never considered myself a fan of chest hair, but Trick's was minimal and *extremely* hot.

"I was gonna wake you."

My fingers clenched in the comforter, lifting it higher to cover my bare breasts as a chill rushed across my skin. "You were gonna wake me... what? Before you bailed out at—" I jerked around to look at my alarm clock. "—four fifteen in the morning?"

That chill turned biting when Trick blew out a deep sigh and dropped his head, reaching up to rub at the back of his neck. The Trick who'd looked at me on that dance floor in a way that made me tremble with desire was long gone. This Trick made my stomach churn while my throat threatened to close up.

"I'm sorry, darlin'," he started uncomfortably, making everything so much worse. "So damn sorry."

I'm sorry. Two words no woman wants to hear after

sleeping with a man she's been crushing on for months and months.

"You're... sorry," I repeated, doing a slow blink as I stared up at him, feeling my heart shrivel up in my chest.

His head shot back up, those piercing gray eyes pinning me to the mattress as if he could hear the heartache in my voice. "I wasn't gonna sneak out, sweetheart. I'd never do that, not to you."

"But...?" I asked, because I just knew there was a *but* coming. I might not have wanted to hear it, but I needed to get this over with. Like ripping off a Band-Aid, swift and without hesitation so he could leave and I could curl up into a ball and have myself a good long breakdown in privacy.

"I shouldn't have done this."

Okay, that *killed*. Squeezing my eyes closed against the onslaught of tears burning my eyes, I turned my head away and pulled in a much-needed breath.

The mattress dipped a second later, and I felt the tips of his fingers under my jaw, turning my face back to his. With no other choice, I opened my eyes and realized I'd gotten it wrong. What I felt a few seconds ago hadn't killed. The guilt in those grays just then did. "I'm so, *so* sorry."

"You said that already," I croaked, my words thick with sadness.

"Because it's true," he responded softly. "You have to believe me, darlin'. I didn't realize I wasn't ready for this until—" He stopped, his throat bobbing with a hard swallow. "I thought I was there, that enough time had passed. You deserve better than what I can give you, Nona. I never would've gone there if—"

"God, please stop." I held my hand up to silence him as my face twisted in pain. His words so far had sliced into me deep enough; I didn't think I could handle anything more. "Just stop. I get it."

"Nona—"

"No, really," I cut in again, this time shoving my way off the bed with the sheet wrapped around me to hide my nakedness. "Like I said, I get it." I began frantically moving around the room, searching for my panties. "Your divorce was basically *just* finalized." I tagged them and struggled to get them up my legs without dropping the sheet. "I totally understand."

"Nona, please just—"

I shuffled toward my dresser, nearly tripping over my own feet. "I should've thought about that. I didn't mean to put you in such an awkward position." I got the drawer open and pulled out the first nightie my fingers landed on, somehow managing to get it over my head and down my body without flashing Trick.

"Sweetheart. If you'd just—"

Now fully clothed, I felt more equipped to handle the crushing blow of rejection he'd just landed. I whipped my hair out of my face and turned back to him, inhaling through my nose in an attempt to calm my frayed nerves.

"Please. Just go," I spoke, my voice weak and quiet, revealing the ache centered in my chest. "Please, Trick."

His face fell, and the sympathy in those stormy eyes nearly did me in. "I don't wanna leave things like this."

My head started bobbing on a nod. "Because you're an amazing man. But I'm asking you, please, just go."

I could see the struggle written all over his face. He didn't want to leave until he was certain I was okay. He was just that good of a guy. Problem was, I didn't think I'd be okay for a good long while, and I needed him *gone* so I could deal with everything I was feeling on my own.

He took a few steps closer, reaching up to place his hand on the side of my neck and brush his thumb across my jaw. As hard as it was—and it was agonizing—I managed to stay still and not flinch away as he took that last piece from me. "You know I care about you, right? That'll never change, Nona."

My head tilted of its own accord, pressing deeper into his touch. "I know." But that knowledge only made me feel worse.

Trick remained unmoving, his eyes scanning every

inch of my face as something played across his features I couldn't even begin to understand. Then, with a gentle, sad smile, he finally dropped his arm, turned to gather the rest of his stuff, and moved out of my room.

I heard the front door close seconds later, and with it, the first tear fell.

CLICK HERE TO KEEP READING

Jessica's Princesses

Come be a part of Jessica's Princesses Reader Group, where you'll get first looks at cover reveals, what's coming next, and so much more.

Jessica's Princesses

About Jessica

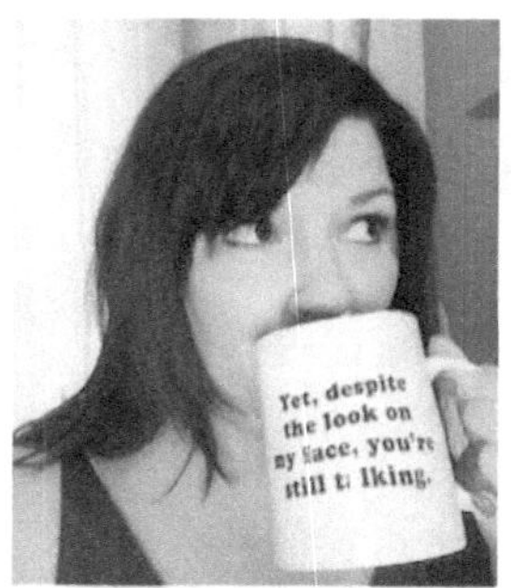

Born and raised around Houston, Jessica is a self proclaimed caffeine addict, connoisseur of inexpensive wine, and the worst driver in the state of Texas. In addition to being all of these things, she's first and foremost a wife and mom.

Growing up, she shared her mom and grandmother's

love of reading. But where they leaned toward murder mysteries, Jessica was obsessed with all things romance.

When she's not nose deep in her next manuscript, you can usually find her with her kindle in hand.

Connect with Jessica now

www.authorjessicaprince.com

Jessica's Princesses Reader Group

Newsletter

Instagram

Facebook

TikTok

authorjessicaprince@gmail.com

www.ingramcontent.com/pod-product-compliance
Lightning Source LLC
Chambersburg PA
CBHW021020310726
48969CB00006B/1466